# Murder in the N

## *Blood on the Page*

## A Psychological Thriller

By Tom McAuliffe

# NEXT STOP PARADISE
# PUBLISHING
Ft. Walton Beach, Florida, USA

100% HUMAN CREATED CONTENT

# Murder in the Margins
## *Blood on the Page*

Printed in the United States of America.
First Edition - 2025

For more information, email:
*BookInfo@nextstopparadise.com*

**Please visit:**
***www.authortommcauliffe.com***

...mai...

...zando in ritardo del tutto. La...
...o in ritardo alla prima...
...che volesse staccargli la...
...ma che brutto carattere. Con...
...l ritardo e l'episodio della scala...

...però quando era in sua compagnia li...
...la sua schiettezza, e il suo entusiasmo...
...me che anche lui aveva per la letteratura...
...lei delle scelte stilistiche degli autori e...
...mplessi di un testo. In realtà, ...
...vocarla. Non riusciva a smettere di...
...so i capelli dal viso, alla sua po...
...flettersi il ginocchio. Chissà se...

# Dedication

To anyone who needs to believe that the past has no sway over the future.

For the love of my life, Sharon.

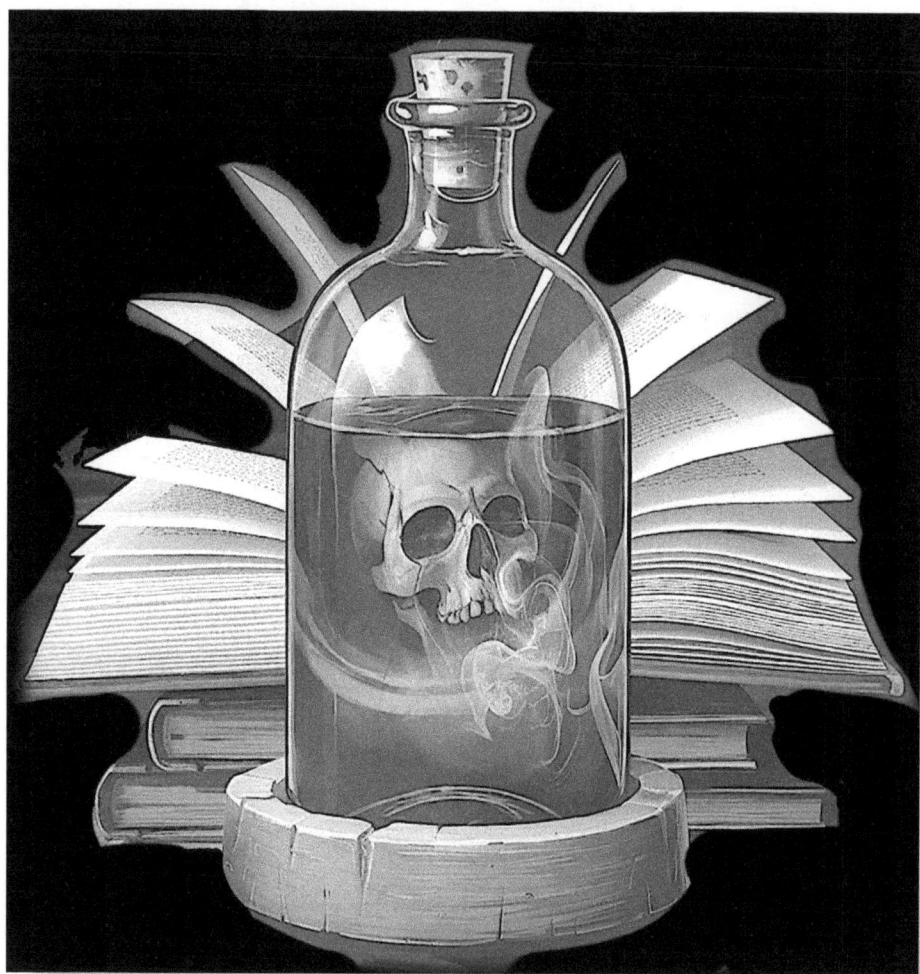

# TABLE OF CONTENTS

# FOREWARD

Ambition is a funny thing. It can make a normal person act crazily and do things that are both ultimately self defeating and alienating to friends and family. If left unchecked it can be a destroyer. Like the music industry the publishing industry harbors some pretty shady characters. It's a competitive and sometimes cut throat world.

The coming of Artificial Intelligence has also affected the creation of books and in this author's opinion has resulted in a significant amount of books on the market that are of lesser quality. To me using ChatGPT is a little like using AutoTune for singing. Shouldn't the singer be able to sing on key? Shouldn't a writer be able to actually write?

Technology today is moving so rapidly we can't keep up. Here for example is the idea of being able to surgically go in and tweak the brain. Doctors can go into the brain and deal with decease and even delete human memories. When, not if, we cross that threshold I feel our society will regret that action. In our story we see that actions have consequences and our pasts will always be with us... forever and unalterable. But do the ends ever justify the means?

Enjoy,

*TOM*

# PREFACE

The house was alive at night.

Morgan stood in the middle of the hallway, the wood beneath her bare feet groaning with every hesitant step. Around her, the air felt thick, the kind of heavy silence that presses against your ears an d your chest. Somewhere behind her, a grandfather clock ticked steadily, its rhythm almost hypnotic. Yet it wasn't the clock that held her attention—it was the door at the end of the hall. It was ajar.

That door had been locked since the moment she arrived. Harper's only rule had been absolute: Don't go in there! The kind of rule that carried no explanation, as though the weight of the edict enough should be obeyed without question. But tonight, it wasn't locked.

A faint light spilled out from the crack under the door, pulsing gently like the glow of a dying ember. Morgan swallowed hard, her mouth dry. She had no reason to be here. No excuse if she were caught. But the door was open, and it was calling to her.

Her pulse quickened as she approached, each step punctuated by the creak of the ancient floorboards beneath her feet. When she reached the threshold, she hesitated, her hand hovering just over the wood. The light inside flickered, shadows dancing along the walls like ghosts. She pushed the door open.

The room smelled of paper and dust, an archive of secrets that had been left to rot in the dark. Bookshelves lined the walls, crammed with journals and loose pages. A desk sat at the center, its surface buried under a chaos of typewritten drafts and photographs. A large stone statue of the flying monkeys from 'Wizard of Oz' stood guard next to the desk with a huge portrait of host Harper behind. And then there was the wall.

At first, Morgan didn't recognize what she was seeing. It was a patchwork of photographs, newspaper clippings, and handwritten notes, all pinned haphazardly in a way that seemed both chaotic and deliberate. Her eyes scanned the collage, piecing together fragments of disconnected lives— smiling faces in faded photographs, articles about accidents and disappearances.

Then she saw it. Her face!

The picture was old, from another life. Morgan at twelve years old, her hair tangled and her smile uneven. It was a candid shot, one she didn't remember being taken. But it was unmistakably her. Beneath the photo, scrawled in Harper's elegant looping handwriting, were two words: 'The Ghost'.

The breath caught in her throat as she staggered back, her hand trembling. Her pulse pounded in her ears as her gaze darted across the wall, desperate for an explanation. There were other notes, more cryptic fragments: Accident. Guilt. Confession.

Her fingers brushed against the edge of the desk, and something clattered to the floor. She looked down. It was a tape recorder, its tiny red light blinking.

Her heart stopped. A voice, soft but unmistakable, filled the room.

"Did you think I wouldn't find you, Morgan?" Harper's tone was calm, almost amused. "You've been running for so long, hiding behind other people's words. But every story needs an ending, don't you think?"

Morgan whipped around, her eyes darting to the open door. The hallway was empty, but she felt Harper's presence everywhere, like a predator circling just out of sight.

"I thought it only fair to let you write your own," the voice continued, crackling slightly through the recorder. "After all, isn't that what you're best at? Giving life to someone else's story while burying your own?"

Morgan's chest tightened. She wanted to run, to leave the house and never look back. But her feet were rooted to the floor, her body frozen by the weight of Harper's words. The recorder, operating automatically, clicked off, leaving her in suffocating silence. And then came the sound. A creak, low and deliberate, from somewhere in the house. Morgan turned toward the hallway, her breath shallow and her skin prickling with fear. Harper was out there somewhere, waiting. Some host.

The gardens were stellar and house seemed to be alive. And Morgan was now trapped inside all of it.

# CHAPTER 1

## The Offer

Claire Morgan had learned to live her life in borrowed voices. A ghostwriter by trade, she spent her days crafting stories for Celebrities, Politicians, Musicians and Authors—names that were household staples, even if their actual words or stories weren't. Her work paid well, gave her the freedom to live on her own terms, and most importantly, kept her anonymous. Morgan liked being invisible on the down low.

But lately, the work had begun to wear on her. Every project felt the same: vain public figures with tedious bullshit stories, desperate to try and sound profound. She spent more time biting her tongue than enjoying the creative process. Yet, she'd long since accepted the trade-off: anonymity in exchange for stability. Invisibility in exchange for distance from a life she didn't want to revisit.

That morning, she sat at her kitchen table, staring at a blinking cursor on her laptop. The draft of her latest project, a memoir for a reality TV personality whose most notable accomplishment was surviving two weeks on a poorly-rated show, remained stubbornly unfinished. A half-empty mug of cold coffee sat next to her laptop. Her phone buzzed on the table, breaking her trance. The caller ID displayed an unknown number. Morgan frowned.

She rarely got calls from unknown numbers—clients usually reached out via email or her agent. Curiosity won out. She picked up.

"Hello?"

"Miss Claire Morgan?" The voice on the other end was crisp, professional, with a clipped British accent.

"This is she."

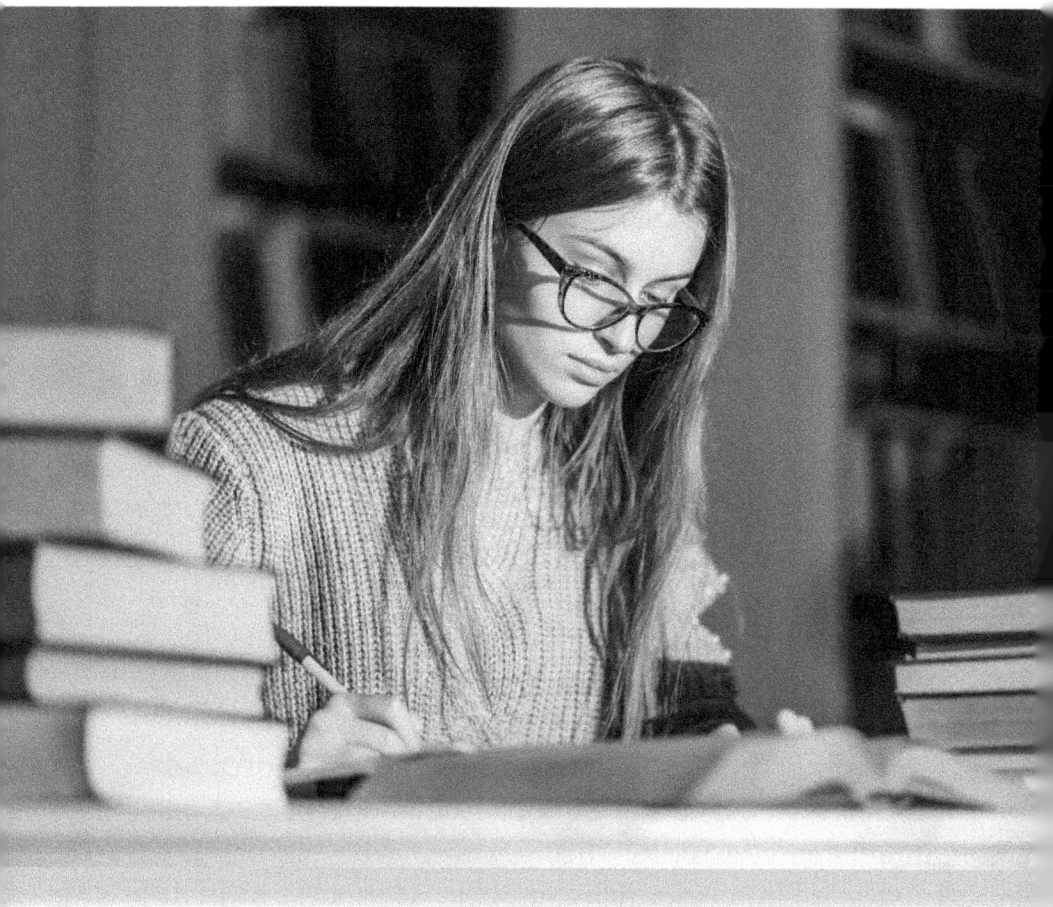

"This is Lucy Hammond," the woman said smoothly. "I'm calling on behalf of Best Selling Author Vivian Harper, my client." She had been the Author's agent and executive assistant for more than 15 years and was partly responsible for her success. She was also fiercely loyal.

Morgan froze. The name was unmistakable. She was well familiar with her, Harper wasn't just an author; she was a literary institution who had come and spoken to her writing class at the University of Michigan almost 20 years ago! Her psychological thrillers had sold millions of copies worldwide, their razor-sharp twists and chillingly realistic characters catapulting her to fame. Harper was also famously private, her public appearances scarce, her interviews non-existent.

"Vivian Harper? Morgan echoed. "Wow she's one of my favorite authors!" she said struggling to mask her surprise.
"Great," Hammond replied. "She's very aware of your work and would like to offer you an exclusive opportunity: to collaborate with her on her memoir."

For a moment, thought she'd misheard. "Her memoir? I wasn't aware she was interested in writing one."

"She hasn't been," Hammond said, her tone precise. "Until now. Harper feels the time is right to tell her story, and she believes you're uniquely suited for the task."

Morgan leaned back in her chair, her mind racing. Vivian Harper's memoir? Wow, that was the kind of project that could make a career. More than that, it could fatten her wallet and elevate Morgan beyond the anonymous world of ghostwriting. But it wasn't just the opportunity that set her on edge—it was the mystery. Why now? And why her? And something about Harper seemed very familiar to her.

"What would this entail?" Morgan asked, her voice cautious.

"Confidentiality is paramount," Lucy said. "You'll be required to sign a non-disclosure agreement before any specifics are discussed. The project may take several months, during which you'll be working exclusively with Harper and to do so you will be staying at her estate outside of New York City. She doesn't travel very much, and she insists on complete control of the environment."
Morgan's eyebrows knit together. Working on-site wasn't unusual for high-profile clients, but being sequestered in a remote mansion for months felt... intense.

"And the compensation?"

Lucy's tone shifted, a subtle smile evident even through the phone. "Substantial. It's a six-figure contract with a deposit when you get started. It's

enough that you won't need to take another project for at least two or three years."

Morgan's fingers tightened around her phone. Substantial could mean anything, but if it was coming from Vivian Harper, it likely meant a life-changing sum.

Still, something gnawed at her. "Ummmm…Why me?" she asked again.

"Simple, she admires your work," Lucy said, her words deliberate. "But I suspect Ms. Harper has her own reasons. Shall I tell her you're interested?"

Morgan hesitated. The thought of working with a literary legend was thrilling, but there was something unsettling about the offer's secrecy. It felt…too good to be true. But the chance to work with Harper, to unravel the mystery of why she had chosen her, and the badly needed money—how could she say no?

"Please tell her I'm very interested," Morgan said.

Three days later, Morgan found herself on the phone with the famous Author Vivian Harper.

"So are you ready to join our little party?" she asked.

"Yes ma'am I'm very excited!" Morgan responded enthusiastically.

"Good. It won't be easy and I'm a bitch to work with," Harper said. "I trust Lucy explained the rules to you?"

"She did mention confidentiality," Morgan said carefully.

"Good," Harper replied, her tone sharp. "But this isn't just about confidentiality. This is about trust. I'm offering you my story, Ms. Morgan. My truth. That is not a responsibility I take lightly, nor should you. Did you sign the NDA… have any questions?"

"Yes I did," responded the young ghostwriter.

"Very good. We have everything you'll need here and I think you will enjoy the estate and be very comfortable. Feel free to use the swimming pool and spa. This is a great opportunity for us both!"

"I'm looking forward to it," Morgan said.

"Good. I will send a Limo for you tomorrow," responded Harper. 'It's about a 3 hour drive so..."

"Great, I look forward to meeting you!" said Morgan. She hung up the phone and found she still had more questions than answers.

The Harper Estate was well-known among literary and media circles for its mystery. It was once owned by famous writer Norman Mailer who had wild parties there during the early 60s. Rumors ranged from orgy's and opulence to eccentricity and an evil ambiance, but no one seemed to know the full truth. As she listen to Harper's words, unease started prickling at her skin. She didn't know what she'd gotten herself into, but one thing was certain: Harper didn't do anything without a reason. And whatever that reason was, she suspected it was going to be more than she'd bargained for. The whole thing had a very sketchy vibe to it.

# CHAPTER 2

## The Arrival

The next day Claire Morgan found herself sitting in the backseat of a black Lincoln Mercury limo, winding through dense woods in mid-state New York south of the 'Finger Lakes'. The road was narrow, flanked by towering pines that seemed to stretch endlessly into the sky. The farther they drove, the more isolated she felt. Morgan shifted uncomfortably in her seat, clutching the signed NDA tightly, and a copy of Harper's last novel—a sharp, brooding masterpiece that Morgan had re-read twice since accepting the job. The trees pressed in closer as the town car ascended the winding road, their gnarled branches knitting together overhead in a canopy that filtered the late afternoon sunlight into fragmented shadows. The occasional flash of the sky through the trees was ominously gray, threatening rain, but not a single drop had fallen. Instead, the air felt charged, thick with the promise of a storm that refused to break.

Morgan sat stiffly in the backseat, her messenger bag clutched tightly against her chest like a shield. The driver hadn't said much since picking her up at the train station. He'd barely looked at her, his face impassive as he loaded her single suitcase into the trunk. Now, as the car turned another sharp bend, Morgan risked a glance at him. His jaw was set, his hands gripping the wheel with the sort of tension that suggested he wanted this drive over as much as she did.

"You've done this trip before?" Morgan ventured, trying to break the silence and make conversation.

The driver glanced at her in the rearview mirror, his eyes shadowed by the brim of his cap. "A few times," he replied curtly, his voice devoid of any real warmth.
Morgan waited for him to elaborate… he didn't.

The car rounded a bend, and suddenly, the estate came into view. It took her breath away. It wasn't just a mansion—it was a fortress!

The road began to level out, and The Harper Estate loomed at the top of a hill, an enormous stone mansion that seemed carved from the same granite cliffs it overlooked. Its slate roof gleamed dully in the fading light, sharp gables and four chimneys stabbing at the sky. Ivy crawled up its façade giving the house an almost organic appearance, as though it had grown out of the earth rather than being built upon it.

"Here we are," the driver said, his voice as flat as his expression. The limo pulled up to the estate.

The wrought-iron gates were massive and ornate, their intricate designs suggesting both wealth and warning. They automatically creaked open as the car approached, the sound reverberating through the otherwise silent grounds. Morgan craned her neck around, noting the way the driveway twisted like a coiled serpent up the hill toward the mansion, flanked on either side by skeletal trees that looked like they might grab at her if she stepped too close.

The estate was sprawling and gothic, its towering sandstone walls lighten with age. Ivy snaked across the facade, and narrow, arched windows glinted in the weak afternoon light like watchful eyes. There were also 4 huge fireplaces. A wrought-iron gate loomed ahead, creaking open automatically as the car approached. Morgan noted the video cameras.

The chauffeur pulled to a stop in front of the main entrance. Morgan climbed out, her boots crunching against the off white gravel. A single lantern above the heavy wooden door cast long shadows across the grand entryway. The main entrance of huge twin oak doors, dark and imposing, stood waiting. No one emerged to greet her. The mansion loomed as if alive, its windows felt like they were like dark eyes watching her, judging her.

"Good luck," the driver muttered as he unloaded her suitcase. His tone suggested she might need it.

"Thanks very much," Morgan replied, but he was already climbing back into the car.

The vehicle disappeared down the drive, leaving Morgan alone. She stared up at the house, its silent grandeur daring her to knock. Before she could summon the courage, one of the heavy oak doors swung open.

Suddenly a well-dressed woman stood in the doorway. She was petite, almost birdlike, with sharp features and an expression that suggested she was not impressed by what she saw nor anything else. Her dark hair was pulled back into a severe bun, and her black dress was impeccably tailored, the kind of outfit that demanded respect—or fear.
"Ms. Morgan," the woman said crisply.

"Yes, hello..." Morgan replied, straightening her shoulders.

"Hi, I'm Lucy Hammond, Ms. Harper's assistant, we spoke on the phone," the woman said. She looked Morgan up and down with a cool detachment that made Morgan feel as though she were being measured for something she hadn't agreed to.

"Please follow me," Hammond said. She turned and disappeared into the house without waiting for a response. Morgan quickly grabbed her suitcase and hurried after her. With a staff of 12... no assistance.

The interior of the house was no less imposing than its exterior. It was cavernous, with high vaulted ceilings and polished wooden or marble floors. A sprawling spiraling staircase filled the foyer. Ancient paintings lined the walls—strange, dark, abstract pieces that seemed to shift under the dim light. The foyer was also breathtaking in its scale and

grandness A massive chandelier hung from the vaulted ceiling, its crystals catching the faint light and scattering it across the dark wood paneling. A grand staircase curved upward, its bannister intricately carved with designs that seemed alive in the flickering glow of the old candle-like lights lining the walls with a huge skylight overhead.

Morgan felt like an intruder, her modest coat and scuffed boots a glaring contrast to the opulence surrounding her. Hammond moved swiftly, her heels clicking against the polished marble floors as she led Morgan through a series of hallways.

"You'll be staying in the east wing," she said without turning around. "The west wing is 100% off-limits."

"Off-limits?" Morgan asked, her curiosity piqued.

She stopped abruptly and turned, fixing Morgan with a look that could have frozen fire. "Ms. Harper greatly values her privacy. You'll respect that, won't you?"

"Of course," Morgan said quickly, though the warning only made her even more curious.

Hammond resumed walking, finally stopping in front of a door at the end of a corridor. She opened it, revealing a large and comfortable room. A four-poster bed with velvet curtains dominated the space, and a writing desk sat near the window, which overlooked the sprawling grounds.

"Ms. Morgan, Dinner is at seven sharp," Lucy said. "Don't be late."

Before Morgan could thank her, Hammond was gone, the door clicking shut behind her.

The room was large and well appointed. The whole damn place felt like the Palace of Versailles! Morgan dropped her bag onto the bed and sank into the calf leather chair by the window. The view was stunning —a wide expanse of manicured gardens giving way to the dark edge of a forest—but something about it felt suffocating. She couldn't shake the sense that she was being watched, though there was no one in sight.

Dinner was an exercise in tension. The door opened before she could knock.

"Ms. Morgan!"

The woman standing in the doorway was petite, with a sharp jawline and piercing blue eyes. She wore a tailored black dress that gave her an air of severe elegance and being way over dressed for this time of day.

"Harper," she said, extending a hand.

Morgan was momentarily struck by how much Harper resembled her public image— uncompromising, powerful, and oddly magnetic. She shook Harper's hand, noting the firm grip.

"It's an honor to meet you," Morgan said.

Harper's lips curved into a faint smile. "We'll see if you still think so by the end of day."

Morgan's stomach tightened. She was not sure if her hostess was kidding or not.
"Please do come in," Harper said, stepping aside and being a good host.

Harper sat at the head of the long oak dining table, a vision of elegance in a dark green silk dress. Her silver-streaked hair was pinned back, and her piercing blue eyes tracked Morgan's every movement as she entered the room. It was all very elegant with the hostess in a full length glitter dress.

"Welcome Ms. Morgan!" Harper said, gesturing to the seat nearest her. "I hope you're finding everything to your liking so far."

"Your home is absolutely incredible," Morgan said, choosing her words carefully as she sat down.

Harper smiled, though it didn't reach her eyes. "It has its charms. I've lived her for almost 23 years."
Dinner was served by two silent staff members, who moved with the precision of a Formula 1 pit crew.

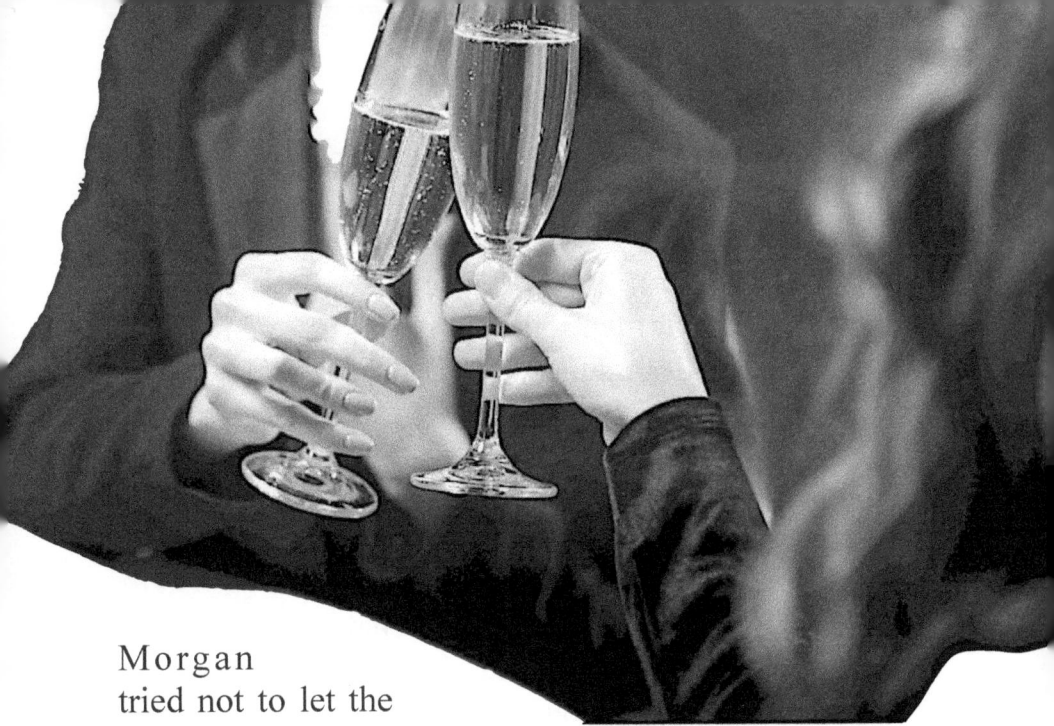

Morgan
tried not to let the
oppressive silence of the
room unnerve her, but it was
difficult.

"I'm curious," Harper finally said, breaking the quiet. "What made you choose this line of work? Ghostwriting, I mean."

Morgan hesitated, caught a little off guard by the directness of the question. "I've always loved helping people tell their stories," she said. "Some people have extraordinary lives but struggle to put their stories into words. I like being the bridge for that," she said.

Harper tilted her head, considering this. "And do you ever wonder if the stories you tell for them are real... are they the truth?"

The question hung in the air, heavy and unanswerable.

"It's not always my job to decide what's true and what's not," Morgan said finally. "In that respect I'm almost like a Journalist, a reporter of facts."

Harper's lips curved into a faint smile. "Good answer. A toast to reporting the facts!" She said raising her Waterford crystal Champagne flute.

After some pleasant dinner chit-chat and a delicious gourmet menu Harper said, "Let me show you my home." She got up from the table.

"This way," she said, her voice soft but direct.

Morgan followed her down a long hallway, her footsteps echoing in the silence. They passed several closed doors, each one identical and unmarked. The air felt heavy, the kind of stillness that carried a quiet warning.

Harper stopped at a pair of double doors and pushed them open. The library was massive, its walls lined with floor-to-ceiling bookshelves crammed with volumes. A grand desk sat in the center of the room, its surface strewn with papers, notebooks, and an old-fashioned typewriter. The room was nothing, if not ornate.

"This is where we'll work," Harper said. "I trust Lucy explained the rules to you?"

"She mentioned confidentiality," Morgan said carefully. "I have the signed NDA."

"Good," Harper replied, her tone sharp. "But this isn't just about confidentiality. This is about trust. I'm offering you my story, Ms. Morgan. My truth. That is not a responsibility I take lightly, nor should you."

Morgan nodded, feeling the weight of Harper's words settle on her shoulders. She was strikingly pretty and moved like a fashion model.

"We'll begin tomorrow morning at 9am sharp," she said. "For now, please settle in. Breakfast is at 7:30 sharp. Please be on time and ready to work."

Without another word, Harper left her in the room alone.

Morgan let out a breath she hadn't realized she was holding in. She wandered over to the desk, her eyes scanning the scattered pages. Most were handwritten notes, their contents cryptic and fragmented. But one page caught her attention. It was a list of names, each one crossed out except for the last: Ms. Vivian Morgan. Beneath it, a single sentence was scrawled in elegant handwriting:

*'I remember her... She'll do nicely'.*

Later that night, Morgan found herself unable to sleep so she began wandering the halls of the mansion. She couldn't sleep, the day's events replaying in her mind like a loop she couldn't escape. The house was silent except for the occasional groan of the old wood under her bare feet, but the stillness didn't feel peaceful. It felt expectant. Her steps carried her toward the west wing almost without her realizing it. She stopped in front of a door at the end of a long hallway, her hand hovering over the doorknob.

"Ms. Morgan?" The voice behind her made her jump. She turned to find the award-winning author standing at the other end of the hall, her expression as sharp as a blade.

"I believe I've made myself quite clear," Harper said, her voice low and stern.

"I'm sorry," Morgan stammered. "I was just... I got lost. I couldn't sleep."
"Curiosity is a very dangerous thing young lady," Harper interrupted. "Especially in this house."

Morgan nodded meekly, her cheeks flushing with embarrassment. "Very sorry." She hurried back to her room, her heart pounding. As she lay in bed, staring at the ceiling, Morgan couldn't shake the feeling that the house was somehow alive and that it had been waiting for her all along. That she was being watched. It was all feeling pretty weird.

# CHAPTER 3

## The First Chapter

The following morning, Morgan woke with a start about 6am, the remnants of her uneasy dreams lingering like cobwebs in the corners of her mind. For a moment, she lay still in the quiet of the room, listening to the house. The occasional creak of timber, the distant shuffle of footsteps, but nothing definitive. It was a soundless kind of presence, an oppressive stillness that seemed to stretch endlessly. The heavy velvet curtains kept the light out, but she could tell by the muted gray glow peeking through the edges and the household sounds that the day had begun.

She swung her legs over the side of the bed and stared down at the dark wood floor. It was cold, almost unnervingly so. Her breath came out in a fog as she stood, smoothing her hands over her pajamas. She had to start working today. There was no way around it. Harper's demands were perfectly clear, even if the atmosphere wasn't. And it was very apparent that she had no tolerance for things she didn't feel important nor of interest to her. She was nothing if not self absorbed.

Morgan's mind wandered to the conversation last night—the one that had started innocently enough but quickly veered into uncomfortable territory. Harper had been more guarded than she had expected. There was something unsettling about the way she'd spoken about truth, about the need for her to prove herself. Morgan had walked away from dinner feeling as though she'd been tested, though she wasn't sure how—or why.

With a sigh, she pushed those thoughts aside and shuffled to the window. The mist from the morning fog clung to the grounds, turning everything in sight into a surreal blur. Somewhere beyond the trees, the sounds of birds had begun to call, a gentle reminder that life, outside of these walls, went on as always.

"Focus, Morgan, focus," she murmured to herself under her breath.

After a solo breakfast that rivaled that of a four-star hotel She made her way back to her room. Harper was no where to be heard from. She decide to get started and sat down at the desk by the window, her fingers grazing the edge of her laptop before she hesitated. No matter how many times she'd started a new project, the first chapter always felt like a sharp knife pressed to her throat—demanding, challenging, almost threatening. But she had a deadline, and Harper strike her as the type to tolerate delays. She needed and wanted to meet her expectations, to prove that she was worth the trust that had been so easily granted and the significant renumeration that was to come.

With a resigned breath, she opened her laptop. The familiar interface of her word processor greeted her, waiting. As always, the blank document seemed to mock her—vast, open, and infinite. But it wasn't the page that intimidated her, no, it was the weight of the story she was about to help shape. She had never ghostwritten a project this crucial or lucrative before. Her previous works had been memoirs, novels, even a few self-help books, but nothing remotely close to the depths of award winning author Harper's life. She was looking forward interviewing Harper.

She clicked on the folder labeled "Project Harper" that had been sent to her and placed on her desktop the day before. Inside was a single file titled The Memoir Draft. She opened it. A series of handwritten pages scanned and converted into digital text filled the screen, each word carrying with it an eerie sense of anticipation. The text was sparse, fragmented. Not yet a story, but a collection of memories, reflections, observations. It was as if Harper had thrown everything onto the page in a fevered burst and then abandoned it, unsure of where to go and what to write next.

Morgan leaned forward, scanning the pages. She'd expected more direction, but the content was an enigma. Harper's 'writer's voice' was unmistakable —sharp, intelligent, and confident—but it was disjointed, as if the story she was trying to tell had been buried for years and only now emerged in small, incoherent bursts. She had to start somewhere. With a steadying breath, Morgan placed her fingers on the keyboard and typed the first few words:

*"The first chapter is always the hardest to write. It's the moment of commitment, when the mind begins to shape the story and the writer realizes the depth of the task ahead."*

She paused, staring at the line for a moment. It felt too perfect, too contrived. But perhaps it wasn't just a good opening—it was a truth. The first chapter always was the hardest. Even in her own work, she had struggled with that same feeling.

She shook her head, backspacing over the line. 'Stop second-guessing. Write the story, Morgan,' she said to herself. She went back to the text from Harper's draft. The next section seemed to chronicle her childhood, but it was disorganized and out of order, full of cryptic phrases, memories without any context. A mess. One sentence Harper had written jumped out at her:

*"I was always alone, even when I wasn't!"*

Morgan's fingers hovered over the keys, considering it. A curious line, but one that suggested more than it told. There was a sadness there, hidden behind the succinct words. Harper had never been one for sentimentality; her strength lay in her ability to hide what mattered most beneath layers of cold logic. But there was no denying the undercurrent of loneliness, something buried in the subtext.

*Clare Morgan fooling around as a 'Ghostwriter'*

She began to type:

*"Loneliness, perhaps, was a gift that came early for me. I never knew the comfort of sibling rivalry, the camaraderie of schoolyard friendships. I was always isolated as a kid, even when I was with others."*

She stopped again, rereading what she had written. It didn't sound like her at all. It didn't even sound like Harper, at least not the sharp, calculating woman Morgan had met yesterday.

But maybe that was the point. Maybe this was the side of Harper that had never been seen, the side that had been buried so deeply beneath her public persona. This, the vulnerability, the isolation—this was what she needed to capture. The real Harper.

41

She continued to write, weaving together the fragments of text from the draft with her own observations, careful to keep Harper's voice alive in every word. The words began to flow more freely now, but Morgan couldn't shake the nagging feeling that she wasn't just writing a story—she was uncovering something far darker, something Harper hadn't really intended to reveal. Other things she pulled from public press reports

By the time Morgan was interrupted, the sun had set and the room had grown cold. She hadn't noticed the time passing, she hadn't noticed the sunlight dimming, or the fact that she hadn't eaten a single thing since she got up. As she typed, she'd been drawn deeper into the story, pulled along by the unspoken truths beneath each line of Harper's text. A knock at the bedroom door jolted her from her trance. She glanced at the clock—nearly seven o'clock! Dinner, no doubt. "Come in," she called, though she wasn't sure if she wanted to be disturbed as she had just gotten up a head of stream writing.
The door opened slowly, and Lucy Hammond stepped inside, her expression unreadable as always. Her eyes flicked over Morgan's cluttered desk, her gaze sharp.

"Ms. Harper is expecting you for dinner," she said, her voice carrying the weight of an unspoken order.

Morgan closed her laptop reluctantly, her fingers lingering on the keyboard for a moment longer before she finally snapped it shut. She could feel the unfinished story tugging at her, the words still circling in her mind. The rough of the first chapter was done, but only just. There was so much left to uncover.

"I'll be right there," Morgan replied, standing up and smoothing her clothes as best as she could.

Hammond didn't respond. Instead, she turned and silently left the room, her footsteps purposeful. Morgan followed her, though her mind kept drifting back to the words she'd written earlier, to the feeling that something was wrong with this story and this situation—something hidden just under the surface.

Dinner that evening was as formal as the night before, though Morgan was less nervous. She had learned to keep her discomfort in check, even as the grand dining room felt as cold and cavernous as ever. The staff moved in and out, placing silver dishes in front of both of them without a word, only the clink of china breaking the silence.
Harper sat across from Morgan, her usual air of calm and control intact, though there was something different in her demeanor tonight. A flicker of something darker—passed across her face when Morgan arrived, but it was gone too quickly to ID.

"Tell me, Ms. Morgan," Harper began, her voice cool and smooth, "how are you finding the writing process?"

"It's going pretty well," Morgan said, trying to sound confident. "The first chapter came together faster than I thought it would."

Harper raised an eyebrow, though she didn't speak. Her silence was as much a tool of interrogation as her words.

"I feel like I'm getting a sense of your voice," Morgan continued. :"and I look forward to interviewing you in more depth. But I'm curious... why did you choose to write this book now?"

Harper's eyes flicked to the side, her fingers drumming lightly against the edge of her wine glass. For a moment, Morgan thought she might not answer. But then, Harper spoke, her voice almost a whisper.

"I'm not getting any younger, Morgan. There are stories that need to be told before it's too late and I'm gone"

Morgan's pulse quickened. There was something chilling in those words, a finality that struck at her core.

"And what kind of stories are those?" the young ghostwriter asked, her voice barely above a whisper.

The veteran Author smiled, though it didn't reach her eyes. "The ones that haunt you, dear. The ones you wish you could forget."

Morgan's stomach churned. She had no idea what she had gotten herself into. The air in the dining room grew heavier as Harper's words hung in the space between them. Morgan's fork, suspended halfway between her plate and her mouth, suddenly felt impossibly heavy. The unspoken tension in Harper's gaze was penetrating and unnerving. She'd expected a certain style from the older woman, a controlled, polished exterior, but there was something behind her eyes now—a flash of something darker almost sinister.

"What do you mean by that?" Morgan finally managed to ask, her voice a little thinner than she intended.

Harper's lips curved upward, but it was not a smile. "You've written enough books to know that there are stories people don't always like to tell," she said, her tone soft but laden with meaning. "They bury them. They lock them away. And sometimes, those stories refuse to stay buried."

Morgan set her fork down slowly, her appetite slipping away like water from her grasp. The atmosphere around them thickened, as though the room itself had taken on an oppressive weight. She had thought this would be a simple assignment—a ghostwritten memoir of a woman with a storied career. Simple. But it was becoming clear that Harper wasn't just a public figure—she was complicated woman with shadows, with parts of her past that she wanted to remain hidden, even if she was the one digging them up.

"I'm not sure I totally understand," Morgan said, her voice quieter now. "Why would you want to bring those negative stories to light? After all this time?"

Harper leaned back in her chair, crossing her arms over her chest. Her gaze never wavered from Morgan's face. "Because some things can't be left in the dark... forever," she said, her voice lowering, becoming almost a whisper. "I've lived my life keeping secrets, but the world isn't what it once was. People are hungry for the truth—no matter how ugly it may be. And I..." She hesitated for just a moment before her voice hardened, the edge returning. "I need to make sure my story is told by me before someone else tells it for me."

The words hit Morgan like a punch to the stomach. She swallowed hard, trying to make sense of the cryptic tone, the weight behind her gaze. The last remnants of her appetite disappeared completely. She didn't want to make too much of it but she thought 'what have I gotten herself into'?

"I think you'll find that writing this book will be… difficult," Harper continued, leaning forward now, her voice steady, almost chilling. "And I'm not talking about the words on the page, Morgan. I'm talking about what happens when you start to uncover the things that were never meant to be uncovered."

For a moment, Morgan considered pushing back, asking what Harper meant. But the words died in her throat, as though something instinctual warned her not to pry. There was a menace to Harper's calm, an undercurrent that Morgan couldn't shake, no matter how hard she tried to ignore it.

Harper studied her for a long moment, then nodded as if she had read Morgan's mind. "You'll understand in time," she said, the coldness returning to her tone. "Just make sure you're ready for it."

Dinner dragged on mostly in silence after that exchange. Morgan pushed the food around her plate absentmindedly, her thoughts churning. She felt like she was drowning in the weight of the conversation, in the strange, unsettling atmosphere of the mansion. It was as if the walls were closing in on her, each passing moment pulling her deeper into a web she hadn't asked to be caught in.

When the meal ended, Harper gave a curt nod, signaling the end of their time together. The staff silently filed in to clear the dishes, and Morgan, feeling small and exposed, stood up to leave. "Well off to write some more," she said.

"I'll see you in the morning, Ms. Morgan," Harper said without looking up from her glass of champaign. "We'll begin the real work tomorrow…"

The words felt like a warning, though she couldn't place why. Morgan nodded stiffly and excused herself. Her feet carried her back down the cold corridors of the mansion, each footstep echoing in the empty hallways. The grand staircase loomed ahead, casting long shadows that seemed to follow her as she ascended toward her room. She continued to be amazed… the place was like a museum.

She got to her room and the door clicked shut behind her with a finality that made her shiver. She stood there for a moment, her hand resting on the cool wood of the door. No turning back now. The project had begun, and Harper's words echoed in her mind: *"The world isn't what it once was."*

What did that mean? What was she hiding? Was Harper's past truly as dark as it seemed? And what was she being asked to uncover? Or was this all paranoia on Morgan's part? Her head spun with questions, but none of them had easy answers. She tried to push the worries aside, telling herself that she was simply overthinking it all—that it was just another gig, another assignment to complete. But deep down, she couldn't shake the premonition that this wasn't like any other book she had ever written.

The night seemed endless. Morgan couldn't sleep. Each time her eyes fluttered shut, the same images kept returning—the mansion, Harper's icy stares, and the unsettling feeling that something sinister lay beneath the surface of this story.

With a sigh, she swung her legs off the bed and wandered over to the desk. Her fingers hovered over her laptop. The first chapter was still not solid, staring back at her, the words seemed like strangers now. The lines she'd written, the reflections she'd crafted in the quiet of the room earlier, now felt incomplete. They were like fragments of a puzzle that she wasn't sure she could ever put together.

But Harper was right about one thing—the first chapter was always the hardest. It was the moment of commitment, the point at which the writer took the plunge into the unknown. And Morgan was already knee-deep into the story at least the research phase. She had turned away other projects and sublet her apartment in the city. She couldn't walk away now. She reopened the draft.

The more she read, the more she began to see patterns. Small details that, when pieced together, told a different story than the one Harper had presented in her notes and the one 15-20 minute exchange they had when she first arrived. A mention of an old family secret. A brief but telling sentence in the notes about a name she didn't recognize but one that lingered in her thoughts. Something about Harper's mother—something that hinted at darkness, a past so carefully hidden, so carefully ignored that it had to be significant.

With trembling fingers, Morgan began to type again, allowing the words to come. She let them flow freely, no longer worrying about structure, no longer questioning herself.

*"In the silence of my youth, I learned the art of deception. I learned how to look others in the eye and tell them everything they wanted to hear, even when my heart screamed the opposite."*

She paused, her eyes scanning the lines. It wasn't

perfect, but it felt real. She had found a voice. Harper's voice.

Morgan leaned back in her chair, staring at the screen. There was something deeply unsettling about these words. The vulnerability they exposed, the raw emotion buried within Harper's guarded exterior, felt like a dangerous path to walk.

But that was what Harper wanted, wasn't it? She indicated she wanted her story to be told, even if it meant digging up the darkest parts of herself. Morgan's fingers hovered over the keyboard again. She wasn't sure where this journey would lead, but she knew one thing for certain—it would be anything but easy. And there was something inside her that couldn't stop herself from writing it. The story, whatever it was, had already begun. She had always looked up to Harper and enjoyed her books.

Morgan was finding it hard to find out her hero wasn't the wonderful woman and author she thought.

The next morning, Morgan didn't feel any more prepared than she had the night before. The manuscript draft she had worked on was now saved and tucked into her bag, and the gnawing sensation in her stomach had only grown worse as the day unfolded.

By the time she entered the grand dining room for breakfast, Harper was already there, sitting at the head of the table with her coffee cup in hand. She looked as composed as always, but this time Morgan noticed something in her posture. It was subtle, but there was a weariness there, something in the way Harper held herself that spoke to years of hidden burdens.

"You're early," Harper said, her tone casual, though the glint in her eye suggested she was anything but. "I like that!"

"I wanted to get an early start," Morgan replied, settling into her seat across from her.

The staff entered with a small spread of breakfast items, and as they worked in silence, Morgan could feel Harper's eyes on her, studying her, weighing her. The last few days had felt like a game of chess —Harper always two steps ahead, Morgan trying to figure out the rules.

"So, tell me," Harper said once the staff had left, her gaze never leaving Morgan's face. "What have you uncovered... I mean accomplished so far?"

Morgan's stomach tightened. There was no turning back now. With a steadying breath, she met Harper's gaze and, for the first time, didn't flinch.

"I've started the first chapter," she said carefully. "But this is more than just the story of your career, isn't it? There's something deeper here. Something... hidden."

Harper didn't answer immediately. Instead, she took a slow sip from her coffee cup, her eyes never leaving Morgan's.

"You're starting to understand," she said, her voice soft, almost approving. "But be careful, Morgan. Some truths are better left untold."

The warning hung in the air between them like a thick fog, impossible to ignore. Morgan's pulse quickened. Whatever Harper's story was, whatever was buried beneath her polished exterior, Morgan was determined to find it. But now, she wondered if, in the end, it would be worth the cost.

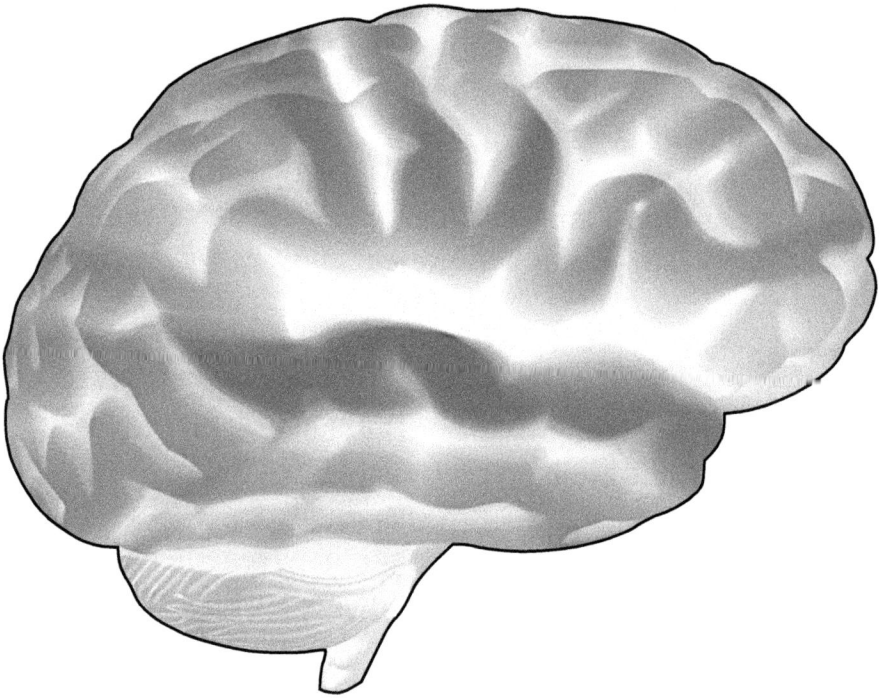

# CHAPTER 4

## The Mind's Escape

The human mind is a fortress of contradictions—both an unparalleled attack tool for survival and a maze of intricate defenses. It can adapt, evolve, and grow in ways that we have yet to fully understand and AI has yet to duplicate. But the brain is also fragile, easily overwhelmed by the weight of experiences that go beyond its ability to process. The mind is capable of remarkable feats of resilience and equally stunning acts of evasion. When faced with horrific events—those that tear at the fabric of a person's soul—it is not uncommon for the mind to retreat, to bury the memories so deep that they are forgotten, or worse, erased.

To Morgan exploring that very phenomenon—the brain's remarkable, yet terrifying, capacity to disconnect from trauma, to shield its owner from unbearable pain, and to reshape reality into something more bearable, was of great interest. To understand how the mind does this, she found that one must look at the mechanics of memory and the ways in which human beings respond to psychological trauma. Memory is not just a passive recording of events; it is an active process, constantly in flux, shaped by emotion, context, and time. And when those memories become too heavy to carry, the mind has its own ways of lightening the load. She studied physiology and psychology in college at the University of Michigan in Ann Arbor where she achieved a dual major BA in psychology and creative writing. She went on to get a Masters in psychology her thesis entitled 'The Architecture of Memory'. Here's what it said...

"To understand how the mind can forget, one must first understand memory itself. Memory is not a simple file stored away in a cabinet, waiting to be retrieved at will. It is a complex process that involves the encoding, storing, and retrieval of information. But this process is far from perfect. The brain's storage system is more akin to a library that is constantly reorganizing itself based on what it deems most important.

At the heart of memory is the hippocampus, a small, seahorse-shaped region of the brain located in the medial temporal lobe. It is responsible for the formation of new memories and the consolidation of short-term memories into long-term storage. When a traumatic event occurs, the brain's usual processes of memory storage can be disrupted. Instead of forming a cohesive, understandable memory, the event is fragmented, disjointed. Sensory details, emotional responses, and contextual information are often scrambled. This confusion allows the trauma to remain unresolved, difficult to grasp.

But it doesn't end there. When an experience is too overwhelming, the brain has a built-in defense mechanism: it can shut down the process of memory formation entirely. The traumatic event may become buried in a part of the brain that no longer has easy access. The conscious mind, then, has no recollection of it. However, the trauma is far from gone—it simply retreats into the unconscious, waiting to manifest in other ways.

One of the most fascinating and chilling aspects of trauma is its ability to leave no direct trace of its occurrence. It is as though the mind, when confronted with an unbearable experience, decides it would be better for the person to simply forget.

This mechanism of forgetting is not an accidental byproduct of trauma, but rather a deliberate, albeit involuntary, response. There are two primary ways in which the brain tries to erase or block traumatic memories: dissociation and repression.\

Dissociation is the process by which a person disconnects from the present moment or from an emotional experience. This is most commonly observed in individuals who have experienced intense or prolonged trauma. The brain, overwhelmed by the event, creates a psychological distance from it. The person may feel as though they are floating outside of their body, watching the event unfold from a distance, or they may experience a sense of detachment from their own emotions.

In severe cases, dissociation can lead to what is known as dissociative amnesia, where an individual is unable to recall specific details of a traumatic event. The memories themselves may still exist, but they are inaccessible to the conscious mind. The brain essentially locks the door to that painful room,

leaving the person with a sense of emptiness or confusion. The event remains buried in the mind, like an old file that the system can no longer access.

While the individual may not remember the traumatic event, the emotions and reactions tied to it can manifest in other ways—through anxiety, depression, or physical symptoms like chronic pain. The repressed memory remains like a shadow, influencing behavior without the person even realizing it." Morgan had wondered how much of her Master's thesis would apply to Harper.She had a feeling a lot of it would. Now with the opportunity to have fully examined the notes and files ands articles Harper had provided her and the one's she had taken, Morgan now had a thesis about Harper. She now believed that she was suffering from some sort of PTSD and had experienced something horrific event in the past either as a witness or as a perpetrator. In her next interview she inquired about that but did not get far with Harper.

"Have you ever had or witnessed a horrific event?" Morgan asked.

"What do you mean?" responded Harper.

"Have you ever killed someone or watched as someone killed a person?" She asked.

"I can't really recall but I think I did have an experience where I witnessed an acquaintance kill someone," she responded.

"That's interesting. People who experience things like that often suffer from dissociative amnesia and repression of memories," explained Morgan. She always enjoyed showing off her Ivy League education. "They may engage in risky behaviors to distract themselves from the underlying emotional pain. The brain may not allow access to the traumatic memory. In fact, repressed memories have been linked to a variety of psychosomatic disorders, where emotional pain is manifest in physical ailments, from chronic headaches to gastrointestinal issues," she explained. Come to find out Harper had all those ailments and more.

"What's your point?" Harper asked.

"Well if something bad has happened in the past, like a murder or rape let's say… it is no wonder we don't remember such things," she said. "It's the minds way of protecting us!"

"There's really no easy answer to the question of

whether forgetting is ultimately a good or bad thing, in many ways, it's just a survival mechanism, a tool the mind uses to protect itself from the overwhelming weight of trauma," Harper related. "And yet, as the mind buries those memories, it risks creating new wounds—emotional, psychological, and physical—that may last a lifetime."

"Indeed. And the mind's attempt to forget can never fully erase the scars of the past. The pain may be dormant, but it is not gone" Morgan added.

"Perhaps the greatest irony is that the more the mind tries to forget, the more it ensures that the memory is never truly gone. It can never be completely erased," Harper offered. "The pain may be hidden, but it will always find a way to resurface, like a tide that can never fully recede."

The interview ended and later as she reviewed the recording and her notes Morgan thought to herself; "The human mind is a paradox. It tries to protect, to shield, to forget—but it can never fully escape its own history. And that history, with all its darkness and light, remains forever imprinted in the deepest corners of the human brain, waiting for just the right moment to re-surface.

"Yeah but, no matter how much we wish to forget," Harper said, "Our past's have a way of catching up and finding us!"

# CHAPTER 5

## The Locked Room

The corridors seemed longer at night, the shadows deeper, the air heavier. Morgans's footsteps were barely audible on the plush runner as she made her way toward the wing Harper had warned her against entering. Something about the restriction gnawed at her. The locked door was a temptation she couldn't resist, its existence as much an enigma as the woman who owned the house. Harper's vague warnings about boundaries and privacy had the opposite effect. They only fueled her curiosity.

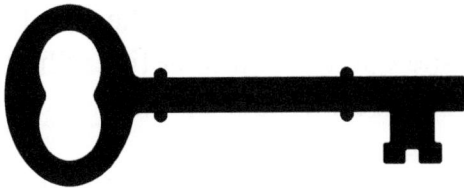

The room was cold and Morgan could see her breath through the moonlight streaming through the narrow windows. It also revealed the intricate woodwork on the door—a design she hadn't noticed during her daytime wanderings. Carvings of ivy snaked up its length, twisting around the heavy brass handle. It seemed both ornate and out of place compared to the rest of the modernized house. Hammond had said the huge carved doors were imported from Italy.

Morgan glanced behind her. The house was quiet, save for the occasional creak of settling wood.

Harper had retired hours ago, and the staff, if they were still around, kept to themselves in the servants quarters. She felt certain no one would find her as she explored. And the urge to discover whatever secrets there were to find was pronounced and compelling her to seek the truth behind the woman.

She reached into her pocket and pulled out the large skeleton key she'd "borrowed" earlier in the day. It had been sitting on a hook in the study, nondescript yet oddly placed, as if daring someone to use it. Her heart thudded against her ribcage as she slid it into the lock. It turned with a reluctant click, the sound echoing in the silence.

For a moment, she hesitated, her hand resting on the door. The air seemed colder here, charged with something she couldn't quite define. She took a deep breath and pushed the door open.

The room was unlike anything Morgan had seen in the mansion. It was huge like most of the rooms with walls lined floor to ceiling with dark, heavy bookshelves. The smell of aged paper and dust hung in the air, mixed with something faintly metallic. A single desk sat in the center of the room, its surface cluttered with scattered papers, an old-fashioned typewriter, and a few framed photographs. A large marble statue of a Flying Monkey from the Wizard of Oz sat next to the desk.

A dim light hung overhead, casting a weak, yellow glow that barely reached the corners of the room. Shadows danced across the walls, giving the space an unsettling sense of movement. Morgan stepped inside, the floor creaking beneath her weight. She left the door slightly ajar, not wanting to risk it locking behind her.

Her eyes were immediately drawn to the photographs on the desk. Most were black and white, faded with time, but one in particular caught her attention. It showed a younger Harper, sitting on a park bench with a man she didn't recognize. Harper's expression was uncharacteristically soft, almost vulnerable, as she gazed at the man. He, in turn, looked at the camera with an easy, confident smile.

Morgan picked up the photo, her fingers brushing the edge of the frame. Who was he? A lover? A colleague? She set it back down and turned her attention to the papers scattered across the desk. They appeared to be drafts of some kind, written in Harpers's meticulous handwriting. The language was dense, filled with cryptic phrases and fragmented sentences that hinted at something deeper, darker.

One line stood out:

*"The truth must never be written, not here, not now, not ever! But it lives inside me. It waits."*

A chill ran down Morgan's spine. What truth? She flipped through the pages, each one more disjointed than the last. Some were half-finished, others marred by violent streaks of ink as if the pen had been pressed too hard. It didn't take long for her to realize that these weren't drafts for her memoir—they were something else entirely. It was as if a cork had popped and all this just streamed out of her.

She reached for another page, but a faint sound stopped her. A creak, soft but deliberate, came from somewhere deeper in the room. She froze, her breath became rapid as she scanned the shadows, her pulse quickening.

"Hello?" she whispered, immediately regretting it. Her voice sounded too loud, too intrusive.

Silence.

She waited, straining to hear anything that might indicate another presence. But the room was still again, the only sound her own shallow breathing. Telling herself it was just the house settling, she turned back to the desk.

That was when she noticed the drawer.

It was slightly ajar, as if someone had accessed it recently. The faint metallic smell she had noticed earlier seemed stronger here. She hesitated before reaching for the handle, her fingers trembling slightly. The drawer slid open with a reluctant groan.

Inside was a small leather-bound journal, its cover worn and cracked with age. It had an intricate design like nothing she had ever seen. Almost satanic. Morgan lifted it carefully, the weight of it unexpectedly heavy in her hands. She knew she was

crossing a line but flipped it open to the first page, her stomach tightening at the sight of the neat, deliberate handwriting.

*"To forget is a luxury I do not have. To remember is a curse I cannot escape."*

She turned the page, her eyes scanning the text. The entries were fragmented, almost like a stream of consciousness but nit as smooth. They spoke of regret, guilt, and a decision that had irrevocably altered the course of her life. But there were no names, no dates—only vague references to events that seemed both personal and monumental.

She was about to turn another page when she heard it again—a creak, louder this time, unmistakable. Her head snapped up, her heart pounding. The shadows in the room seemed to shift, as if something or someone was moving just out of sight.

"Who's there?" she demanded quietly, her voice steadier than she felt.

No answer.

She stood, clutching the journal tightly, her eyes darting around the room. The dim light overhead flickered, plunging the room into momentary darkness before returning to its weak glow. The air felt thicker now, pressing against her like an unseen force.

Morgan backed up toward the door, her instincts screaming at her to leave. But as she reached for the handle, her foot brushed against something on the floor. She looked down and saw a faint, dark stain seeping into the wood—a stain that hadn't been there before. Was it Blood?

Her breath caught in her throat as her sight followed the trail, which led toward the far corner of the room. The shadows there seemed impossibly dark, almost alive. She swallowed hard, every nerve in her body on edge.

Against her better judgment, she stepped closer, the journal still clutched in her hand. The trail ended at the base of one of the bookshelves, which, up close, looked slightly misaligned compared to the others. She reached out, her fingers brushing against the edge of the shelf. It moved.

The sound of grinding wood filled the room as the bookshelf slid open, revealing a narrow secret passageway shrouded in darkness. The metallic smell was stronger now, almost overwhelming. Morgan hesitated, her instincts warring with her curiosity. But something compelled her to step forward, to see what lay beyond. Another part of her thought she was nuts!

The passage was cold, the walls rough and unfinished. A faint light flickered at the end, casting long, shifting shadows. Morgan moved cautiously, her footsteps muffled by the narrow space. The air grew colder with each step, and the metallic smell turned sharper, mingling with something else— something acrid, musty and foul.

At the end of the passage was a small, dimly lit room. It was stark and utilitarian, a stark contrast to the opulence of the mansion. The walls were lined with metal shelves, each one cluttered with old files,

photographs, and objects that looked like relics from another time. In the center of the room was a single chair, its leather seat cracked and worn, with heavy restraints attached to the armrests and legs. It appeared to be a converted Dentist chair.

Morgan's stomach turned as she took in the scene. This wasn't just a hidden room—it was something far darker, far more sinister. The chair looked like it had seen years of use, and the blood stains on the floor beneath it told a story she didn't want to imagine.

Her gaze fell on a file sitting open on one of the shelves. She approached it hesitantly, her fingers trembling as she reached for it. The file contained photographs—grainy, black-and-white images of people she didn't recognize. Some looked terrified, others defiant, but all of them had the same haunted look in their eyes.

Beneath the photographs were documents, their text heavily redacted. But one phrase stood out, repeated over and over again: "Project Mnemosyne."

"What the hell is this?" Morgan whispered to herself, her voice barely audible.

The sound of footsteps behind her sent her heart into her throat. She spun around, her back pressing against the shelf. The passageway was empty, but she could feel it—someone was there, watching "Morgan." The voice was low, almost a whisper, but unmistakable, it was Harper. Morgan's pulse raced as her figure stepped into the room, her silhouette sharp against the dim light. Harper's expression was unreadable, her eyes cold and calculating as if she expected this to happen.

"I told you to stay out of this part of the house," Harper said, her tone calm but laced with menace. "You should have listened."

Morgan swallowed hard, her mind racing for an explanation. "I got lost. I, I was just—"

"Curious," Harper finished for her. She took a step closer, her gaze fixed on the journal still clutched in Morgan's left hand. "Curiosity is a dangerous thing, Morgan. Especially in this house."

Morgan tried to speak, but the words wouldn't come. The room seemed to close in around her, the shadows pressing against her like a living force

"You've seen too much," Harper said, her voice soft but deadly. "And now, I'm afraid, you'll have to understand the price of knowing."

The door to the passageway slammed shut, plunging the room into total darkness. Morgan's scream was swallowed by the shadows, her mind racing about the truth she may have uncovered began to unravel. And in that moment, she realized that whatever secrets her host was hiding, they were far more dangerous than she could have ever imagined.

# CHAPTER 6

## The Newspaper Clipping

The envelope was unmarked, no stamp, no return address, only her name scrawled in thin, deliberate handwriting across the front: Morgan Ashton. It had been slipped under her bedroom door sometime during the night, and she found it just as dawn's pale light began to seep through the tall windows.

Morgan held it in her hands now, her thumb tracing the indentation of her name. The paper was smooth, but there was something faintly greasy about it, as though it had been handled too many times before reaching her. Her heart quickened. Was this Harper's doing? A warning? An invitation?

She hesitated for a moment before tearing it open. Inside was a single piece of yellowed newsprint, brittle at the edges as though it had been ripped from an old newspaper. No note accompanied it, no explanation—just the clipping. She unfolded it carefully, her eyes scanning the bold, faded headline.

*September 14, 1997*
*MYSTERIOUS DISAPPEARANCE OF LOCAL JOURNALIST SPARKS FEAR*

Beneath the headline was a grainy photograph of a man in his late thirties, wearing wire-rimmed glasses and a hesitant smile. His face was familiar in the way strangers sometimes feel—like a face you've passed once in a crowd or glimpsed on a train yet is stuck in your memory. Morgan's stomach twisted as she read on;

*'Matthew Grayson, a respected journalist and investigative reporter, vanished without a trace late last week. Known for his hard-hitting exposés and fearless pursuit of truth, Grayson was last seen leaving his home in Hawthorne Ridge on the morning of September 10th. Neighbors reported no unusual activity, and police have found no evidence of foul play—yet suspicions grow.*

*Sources close to Grayson suggest he had been working on a sensitive story before his disappearance, though the nature of the investigation remains unknown. His family, visibly distraught, have appealed to the public for any information that might lead to his whereabouts.*

*"He wouldn't just leave," said Amelia Grayson, his wife of twelve years. "He's been under a lot of stress because of his work, but he wouldn't abandon his family."*

*Police asked anyone with information to come forward, but as the days stretched into weeks, hope faded. Grayson's editor described him as 'a relentless truth-seeker' and suggested his disappearance could be linked to his work. Rumors swirl about a story so explosive it could have put him in danger, though no concrete evidence has surfaced.*

*Grayson is the third journalist to vanish in the past five years under similar circumstances, a chilling trend that has sent shockwaves through the local press community. For now, the mystery remains unsolved, leaving his family—and the truth—dangling in the balance.'*

Morgan's hands trembled as she read the final words. She turned the clipping over, but the back offered nothing more than faded classifieds, selling old appliances and offering handyman services. Her heart raced as she tried to process what she had just read. Why had it been left? What did it all mean?

The name didn't ring any bells, and yet the edges of her mind seemed to itch with familiarity, as if she should know something about Matthew Grayson but couldn't quite place it. Was this tied to Harper? To her memoir? She again had more questions than answers.

The events of the previous night flooded back—the locked room, the bloodstained floor, the hidden passage. The memories felt disjointed, like they belonged to a nightmare rather than something she had lived. But the heaviness in her chest told her otherwise. Whatever Harper was hiding, it was far darker than anything she had imagined. And this clipping—this journalist—felt like another thread in a web she was only beginning to see.

She folded the clipping carefully and slipped it into the pocket of her robe. A knock at the door startled her, and she instinctively pressed a hand over her pocket as though it could shield the secret she had just uncovered.

"Morgan?" Harper's voice was sharp and clipped, no trace of the warm hostess who had greeted her days before.

Morgan's breath hitched. "Yes?"

"Breakfast is ready," she said. "Please join me in the dining room."

"Of course," Morgan managed, her voice steady despite the rapid pounding of her heart. She was also a bit confused as she hadn't realized it was morning.

Harper didn't wait for a response. Morgan heard her footsteps retreat down the hall, slow and deliberate.

The dining room was suffused with morning light, the long table set with a modest spread of fruit,

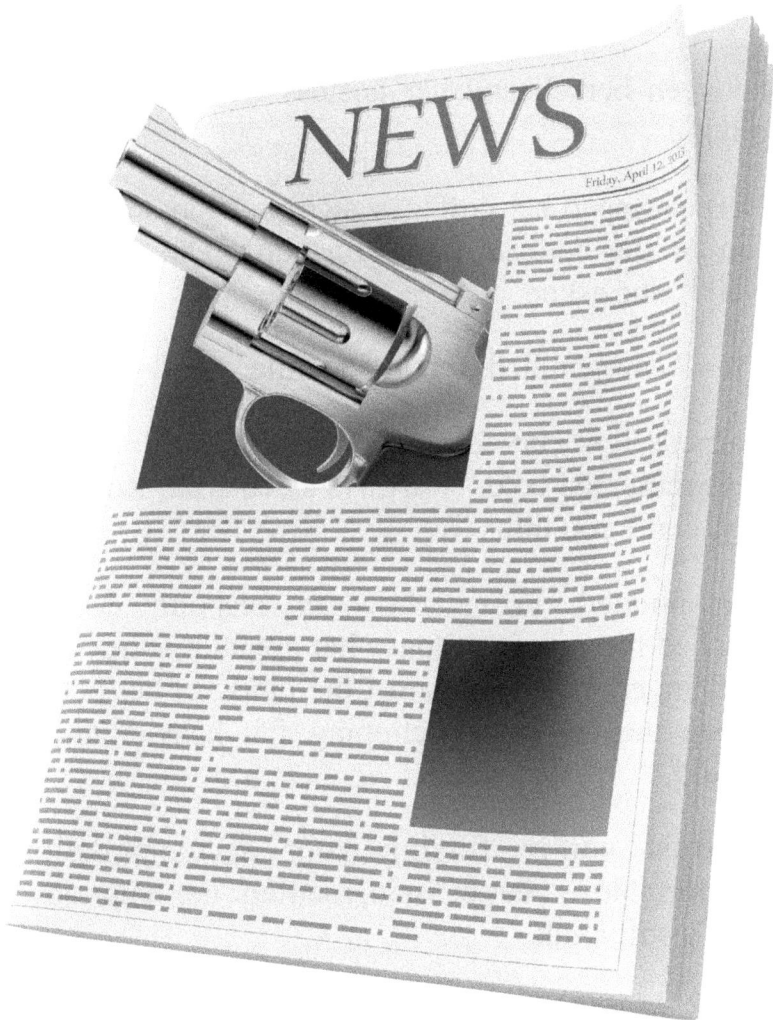

toast, pastries and coffee. Harper sat at the head, her posture as rigid as the high-backed chair she occupied. She glanced up as Morgan entered, her expression unreadable.

"Good morning," Harper said, her tone polite but distant.

"Morning." Morgan took a seat several spaces down, putting as much distance as she could between herself and her hostess without making it obvious.

Harper sipped her coffee, watching Morgan over the rim of the delicate porcelain cup. "Did you sleep well?" she asked.

"Yes," Morgan lied, forcing a smile. "And you?"

Harper's lips curved into a faint smile, though her eyes remained cold. "I always sleep well. Routine is key, don't you think?"

She nodded, unsure how to respond. Morgan reached for a piece of toast, her appetite nonexistent. Her fingers brushed against the fabric of her pocket, where the newspaper clipping felt heavier than it should.

"I trust you're finding your accommodations comfortable," Harper said, setting her cup down with a soft clink.

"They're lovely," Morgan said quickly. "Thank you again for your hospitality."

Harper leaned back in her chair, her eyes never leaving Morgan. "I hope you haven't been wandering too much. This house has a way of... overwhelming guests who stray. Some get lost never to be heard from again..." she said with a little chuckle.

But the words hung in the air like a warning. Morgan forced another smile, her heart hammering

76

in her chest. "I've been staying close to the library," she said.

"Good," Harper said, her smile sharpening. "The library is... safe."

Morgan's grip on her fork tightened. Was that a threat? A warning? A test?

Harper stood abruptly, smoothing the folds of her immaculate dress. "I have some matters to attend to in town this morning, but we'll meet in the study later. Say around 4ish? I'd like to review your notes and progress on the memoir."

"Of course," Morgan said, nodding.

Harper's heels clicked against the polished floors as she left the room, her presence lingering long after she was gone. Morgan waited until she was sure Harper was out of earshot before pulling the newspaper clipping from her pocket. She studied it again, searching for clues she might have missed the first time. The name of the town—Hawthorne Ridge—jumped out at her. She had seen it before, somewhere in the stacks of Harper's personal files. Did she have something to do with this disappearance? She needed more information, and she knew where to start.

The study was empty when Morgan entered, the scent of leather and aged paper filling the air. She moved quickly to the filing cabinet in the corner, where Harper had stored years' worth of documents, notes, and drafts. Her hands trembled as she rifled through the folders, her eyes scanning for anything that might connect to Journalist Matthew Grayson.

It didn't take long to find it. A folder labeled 'Hawthorne Ridge, 1997' sat near the back of the file drawer. She pulled it out and placed it on the desk, her breath halting as she opened it.

Inside were photographs, maps, and pages of typed notes. The photographs were similar to the one in the newspaper—a young Harper, her expression unreadable, standing beside a man who Morgan now recognized as...Matthew Grayson. They looked happy, but there was an undercurrent of tension.

The notes were more cryptic. Phrases like "Witness unreliable" and "Evidence destroyed" appeared repeatedly, along with references to something called 'Project Mnemosyne'. Morgan's mind raced as she pieced the fragments together. Matthew Grayson hadn't just been working on a sensitive story—he had been investigating... Harper. Whatever he'd uncovered cost him everything including his life.

'Project Mnemosyne' was, no pun intended, a cutting edge effort to explore the human brain through surgery and in particular its responses to

sexual stimuli. In Greek mythology, 'Mnemosyne' is the 'Goddess of Memory' and the mother of the nine Muses by her nephew the greek god Zeus. It appeared that the effort went on for 5 years with as many deaths. The bodies were not found... the bones were through.

A faint noise outside the study made Morgan freeze. She shoved the folder back into the drawer closing it quietly, her pulse racing. Footsteps approached, slow and deliberate. The door creaked open, and Harper walked in, her expression as calm as ever.

"Looking for something?" she asked, her tone light but laced with suspicion.

Morgan forced a smile, her heart hammering. "Just trying to get a head start on the memoir."

Harper's eyes narrowed slightly, her eyes lingering on the filing cabinet. "I see," she said. "I hope you're finding everything you need."

Morgan nodded, willing her hands to stay steady. "Yes, it's all very helpful."

Harper smiled faintly, though her eyes remained cold. "Good. I'd hate for you to feel... lost." She turned and left the room without another word, leaving Morgan to catch her breath. But the warning was clear: somehow Harper was watching, and she knew far more than she let on.

Morgan glanced back at the filing cabinet, her resolve hardening. Whatever the veteran author was hiding, it was bigger than anything she could imagine. But she knew there was something. And if Matthew Grayson had risked everything to uncover some important truth, she owed it to him—and herself—to do the same.

But one thing was certain: the closer she got to 'the truth' whatever that was to be, the more dangerous things felt.

# CHAPTER 7

## The Unfinished Manuscript

The house was utterly silent except for the faint creak of the floorboards beneath Morgan's slippers (a present from her host). It wasn't a sound she would have noticed during the day, but at night, when the mansion's ancient walls seemed alive with whispers and groans, every step felt amplified. Her fingers tightened around the flashlight as she slipped into the study, her heart hammering in her chest. This was madness.

She had come to believe that Vivian Harper was dangerous—Morgan had no doubt of that now. All she lacked was… evidence. The redacted manuscript among the provided documents, the references to Matthew Grayson, and the locked room had made it abundantly clear that something was being hidden. And yet, here she was, sneaking through the darkened halls of Harper's estate, driven by a compulsion she couldn't entirely explain. Had she become a professional snoop?

The provided manuscript wasn't just an attempt at a memoir. It was a confession, a riddle, and a threat all rolled into one. And whatever secrets it held, Morgan needed to uncover them before Harper turned her calculating gaze fully on her.

She froze as the study door creaked softly under her touch. Inside, the room was cloaked in shadows, the moonlight barely piercing the heavy curtains. She scanned the desk with her flashlight, expecting to see the manuscript where she had left it earlier that day. But it was gone!

Her stomach sank as the flashlight beam swept over the empty surface. Harper must have moved it. The realization sent a chill down her spine. If Harper had taken the manuscript, it meant she knew the writer was prying deeper than she was meant or authorized to.

Still, Morgan wasn't ready to back off let alone give up. She turned her attention to the bookshelves, running her fingers along the spines as she searched for any sign of the manuscript. Nothing. She checked the drawers of the desk next, but they were locked. She even looked under the desk, as absurd as that seemed.

That's when she noticed the faint glow of light seeping out from under a door further down the hallway.

Morgan hesitated, her mind racing. She hadn't explored that part of the house yet, but she was sure the light hadn't been there before. V Harper's warning echoed in her mind: 'Some truths are better left buried.' But she couldn't stop now.

The door led to a room she hadn't seen before, smaller and colder than the study. The walls were

plastered with photographs, newspaper clippings, and handwritten notes pinned in haphazard clusters. A single desk sat in the center, and there, resting in the middle of the clutter, was the manuscript.

Morgan's breath doubled as she stepped inside. The air was heavy with the scent of dust and something faintly metallic. Her eyes darted to the walls, taking in the chaotic arrangement of images and text.

Photographs stared back at her—black-and-white, grainy shots of people she didn't recognize. Each face was accompanied by a name and a date scribbled in pencil beneath it. Some of the dates were crossed out in heavy, angry slashes, while others were circled.

She leaned closer, her stomach twisting as she read the dates. They weren't random; they were disappearances. Missing persons. Her look shifted to the clippings, her flashlight illuminating headlines like:

*"Journalist Vanishes While Investigating Local Estate"*

*"Third Missing Person in Hawthorne Ridge Sparks Fear"*

*"Authorities Baffled by String of Unsolved Disappearances"*

Each article mentioned names—names that matched the ones beneath the photographs. And then, in the corner of one board, she saw it: Matthew Grayson.

The grainy photograph from the newspaper clipping was pinned there, his hesitant smile now seeming like a warning. Beneath his name, the date September 14, 1997 was circled in red.

Morgan's pulse quickened as she turned back to the desk. The manuscript was open to a page near the middle, the words written in Harper's precise, almost mechanical handwriting style.

"The mind is a malleable thing. Memories can be rewritten, erased, replaced. But there is always a cost. The cracks, though small at first, eventually deepen. And sometimes, what we bury doesn't stay buried."

Morgan's breath hitched. She flipped back a few pages, her fingers trembling. The earlier sections had been largely redacted, but here, the text was intact.

"Matthew Grayson came too close to the truth. He was relentless, and for that, he paid the ultimate price. But even now, his shadow lingers, a reminder that some stories are better left untold."

She stared at the words, her mind reeling. Matthew Grayson hadn't just disappeared—he'd been silenced. And Harper was admitting it, right here, in her own words.

But why? What truth had he uncovered that was worth killing for?

The sound of footsteps in the hallway snapped Morgan out of her thoughts.

She froze, her heart pounding as the steps drew closer. They were slow and deliberate, each one echoing louder than the last. She scrambled to close the manuscript, her hands fumbling as she tried to tuck it back into the pile of papers on the desk. The footsteps stopped just outside the door. She backed away, her flashlight trembling in her grip. The door creaked open, and Harper walked in.

She was dressed in a long, dark robe, her hair perfectly arranged despite the late hour. Her eyes swept over the room, landing on Morgan with an intensity that made her stomach churn.

"You shouldn't be here," Harper said, her voice calm but laced with an undercurrent of menace.

"I... I was looking for—"

"For what?" Harper interrupted, stepping closer. "Answers? Closure? The truth?"

Morgan swallowed hard, her mind racing for an explanation.

Harper's gaze shifted to the manuscript on the desk. Her expression darkened. "Ah. You've been reading."

"I... I was just trying to understand," Morgan stammered.

Harper smiled faintly, though her eyes remained cold. "Understand what? That some stories are better left untold? Or that some truths will only hurt you?"

Morgan's back pressed against the wall as Harper stepped closer, her presence suffocating.

"You think you've uncovered something significant," Harper said, her voice low and steady. "But you don't know the half of it. You don't understand what you're meddling with. This is not part of the book."

Morgan's breath galloped. "Then please explain it to me," she said, her voice trembling.

Harper tilted her head, studying Morgan as though weighing her options.

"Very well," she said finally. "But remember this: once you know the truth, there's no turning back. You can't unhear or unknown something young lady. Just make sure you want to know, ya know?"

Harper moved to the desk, her fingers brushing over the manuscript with a strange reverence.

"This," she said, gesturing to the pages, "is more than a memoir. It's a map. A record of the choices I've made, the sacrifices I've endured. And the possible consequences of…"

Morgan watched as Harper flipped through the pages, her movements precise and deliberate.

"Matthew Grayson," Harper said, her voice softening. "He was a brilliant man, but he didn't know when to stop. He uncovered something he shouldn't have, something that put everything at risk."

"What... what did he find?" Morgan asked, her voice barely above a whisper.

Harper's stair locked onto hers, and for the first time, Morgan saw something resembling vulnerability in her eyes.

"Memories," Harper said. "Memories that don't belong to him. Memories that didn't belong to anyone."

Morgan frowned, confused. "I sorry I don't understand."

Harper sighed, her shoulders sagging slightly. "You will," she said. "But not tonight."

Before Morgan could respond, Harper snapped the manuscript shut and turned to leave, her robe billowing behind her like a royal cape.

"Go to bed, Morgan," she said over her shoulder. "You'll need your rest for what's to come."

Alone in the room, Morgan stood frozen, her mind racing with questions. Whatever Harper was hiding, it was far more dangerous—and far more personal— than she had imagined. And as she stared at the manuscript, the unfinished confession that seemed to hold all the answers, she knew two things for certain: Harper wasn't just an award winning author and she was hiding something. She was a keeper of secrets both hers and others. And laying in a bed made in 1908, Morgan now understood she was entangled in a story far darker than she imagined.

# POISONS

UNDER the name of poisons we include all bodies, solid, liquid, or gaseous, which are capable of acting upon the human system in other than a mechanical way, so as to produce injury or death.

The substance may produce its effects either by a chemical action on the tissues of the body, or by a physiological action from absorption into the living system.

When, after eating or drinking, a person is suddenly seized with severe pains in the stomach, with vomiting, followed by inclination to sleep, or by convulsions, or great prostration, or nervousness, we suspect at once that some poison is acting upon the system. So numerous are the poisons existing in nature, and so extensively are many of the most powerful ones used in the arts and industries, that it is a matter of surprise that fatal poisoning is not more frequent.

Poisons may be divided into irritants and narc_____ nitric acid, and caustic potash being examples _____ opium, alcohol, and strychnia, of poisons are _____

Some poisons are fatal when _____ hers are in co_____ whereas others are in constant _____ well-being, be_____ sary to his well-being, becoming bad, or in very l_____ concentrated, or in very large qua_____ a grain of a_____ fraction of a grain of atropine, _____ nightshade) may cause death wit_____ may cause deat_____ carbonic-acid gas, which exis_____ acid gas, which exis_____ breathe, if inhaled in their pure _____ inhaled in their pure _____ duce poisonous effects. So it is w_____ onous effects. So it is w_____ nature, and made use of in so_____ and made use of in some w_____ able medicines we possess ar_____ icines we possess are su_____ _____emselves poisonous, may be giv_____ poisonous, may be giv_____ _____n becomes a great boon to humanity._____ _____rain, many articles of food contain potent poisons,_____ _____ and combinations that we could not w_____ _____u.

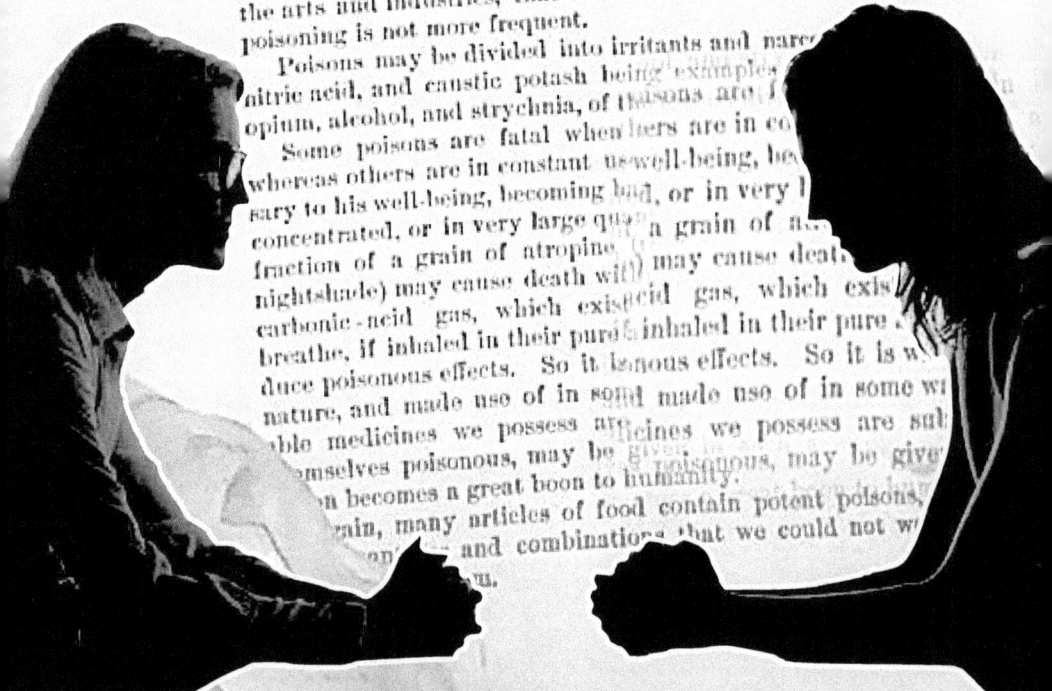

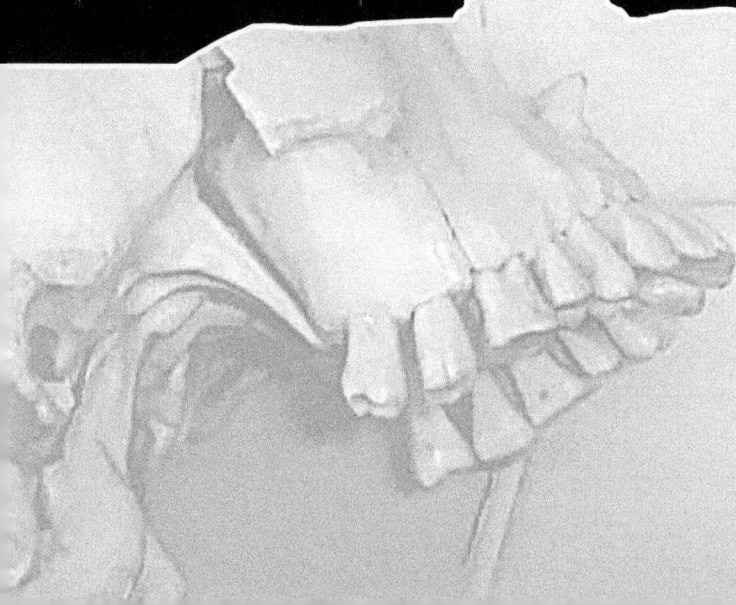

_____ will first_____

There are certa_____ ous and irritant pro_____ surface of the body._____ produce depends upo_____ susceptibility of the s_____ able to handle these po_____ effects, while others ha_____ the neighborhood of a _____ ing.

The princi_____

# CHAPTER 8

## The Confrontation

The storm outside seemed almost alive, clawing at the windows of the Harper estate with relentless fury. Each crack of thunder rattled the ancient glass, the vibrations echoing through the cavernous dining room where Morgan sat facing Harper. The air between them was charged, heavy with the weight of truths left unspoken for far too long.

Harper, ever poised, reclined in her chair, her fingers wrapped around a wine glass. Her calm demeanor, polished as always, was a mask—Morgan was now certain of it. Beneath the surface, Harper was a woman accustomed to controlling things, and it was obvious that Morgan's probing questions had begun to unsettle her.

"I must say," Harper began, her voice smooth but laced with a faint sarcasm, "I do admire your curiosity. It's what makes you such a talented writer. But there is a fine line between curiosity and recklessness, Morgan. Have you considered which side you're standing on?"

Morgan stared at the older woman, her grip tightening on the folder she'd brought with her. "I've crossed that line already," she said. "And I'm not going back. You said you wanted a book that was 110% honest look at your life… right?"

'Not everything. Some things are too... too delicate for the public to hear. I mean it's one thing for you and I to sit here and chat but quite another to walk into a bookstore and see it available for the masses. They'd never understand," she said.

"Then please help me understand," Morgan responded. "I know you don't want a book filled with fluff... right?"

"Correct" she said curtly as she sipped her drink.

Morgan opened the folder, revealing the photographs and newspaper clippings she had collected during her clandestine searches through Harper's hidden room. Each piece of evidence was a crack in the carefully curated façade Harper had spent decades building.

"Matthew Grayson," Morgan said, sliding a newspaper clipping across the table. The headline screamed up at them both:

*'Local Journalist Missing: Investigation Stalled.'*

"Do you know who killed him?" she asked.

No response.

Harper's expression didn't falter, but the faint twitch of her lips betrayed her. Morgan pressed on, her voice steady despite the storm raging in her mind.

"Then there's Eleanor Tate," Morgan continued, placing another clipping on the table. "And Alan

Fraser. And those photos in the hidden room. All those faces, all those names—they're not just coincidences, are they? Not just friends?"

Harper leaned back in her chair, her eyes narrowing. "You've certainly been very busy," she said, her tone light but her words cutting. "But do you truly understand what you've uncovered? You don't!"

Morgan leaned forward, her pulse quickening. "I understand enough," she said. "Enough to know you're not just an eccentric award winning Author with a tragic past. You're hiding something. Something dark. I'm afraid that if I go further y9ou are not gonna like the results."

Harper's smile was faint, but her eyes were sharp as razors. "Everyone has skeletons in their closet, Morgan. Even you!"

Morgan ignored the jab. "This isn't about skeletons. It's about lives—people you've silenced, stories you've erased. Why? Am I wrong? What's so important that you'd destroy anyone who gets close to it?"

The room seemed to grow colder as Harper stood, her movements deliberate. She crossed to the window, her silhouette outlined by the flickering lightning outside.

"You think you've uncovered some grand conspiracy," Harper said, her voice low. "But the truth is far more complicated—and far more dangerous—than you can imagine."

Harper turned back to face Morgan, her expression unreadable. "You're not the first to come looking for answers," she said. "And you won't be the last. But let me offer you a piece of advice: some truths are better left buried. And this is not something to be made public."

Morgan pushed her chair back, the screech of wood against stone breaking the tense silence. "That's not your decision to make now," she said. "You don't get to decide who deserves the truth. Our contract does not allow you to edit and delete facts. But this is your opportunity to set the record straight with the truth."

Harper's look hardened. "And what will you do with the truth, Morgan? Publish it? Turn it into another sensationalist story for people to consume and destroy my life? You think you're different from the others, but you're not. You're just another scavenger, trying to make a buck picking at the bones of something you don't understand."

Morgan felt anger and fear warring within her. "Then explain it to me," she said. "Please help me understand."

Harper studied her for a long moment, the storm outside casting eerie shadows across her face. Finally, she sighed, the weight of years now etched into her features.

"Follow me," she said.

Morgan hesitated as Harper led her down a narrow stone stairway, the walls lined with faded portraits of long-dead friends and family. The air grew colder the deeper they went, and Morgan's stomach filled with unease. They stopped in front of a door Morgan hadn't noticed before. Harper produced a large key from her pocket and unlocked it with a click.

"This is where it all began," Harper said, pushing the door open.

The room was vast and sterile, its white walls and bright fluorescent lights a jarring contrast to the rest of the mansion's gothic charm. Shelves lined with binders and stacks of papers filled the space, but it was the object in the center of the room that drew Morgan's attention.

A sleek metallic device sat on a steel table, wires and electrodes snaking out like the limbs of some mechanical beast.

"What is this?" Morgan asked, her voice trembling a bit. It looked weird.

Harper approached the device, her movements reverent. "This," she said, "is the culmination of years of research—of sacrifice. It's a tool for rewriting the mind, Morgan. Memories can be erased, altered, replaced entirely. Pain can be removed, trauma healed. It's a revolution."

Morgan took a step back, her pulse racing. "You used this on people," she said. "That's what the photographs are, aren't they? Your… test subjects."

Harper's expression tightened. "They volunteered," she said. "At first."

Morgan's breath caught. "At first?"

Harper's silence was answer enough.

The storm outside roared louder, the wind slamming against the windows like a beast trying to break in. Morgan's voice rose above the noise, her anger spilling over.

"So you didn't really heal people," she said. "This thing erased them? Matthew Grayson, Eleanor Tate

—they didn't just disappear. You made them disappear."

Harper's composure cracked, her voice rising in defense. "You think this was easy?" she snapped. "All I wanted to do was write! You think I enjoyed making those choices? This technology has the power to change the world, to rewrite the worst parts of our lives. But progress comes at an enormous price."

Morgan shook her head, the potential of tears of frustration now burning the edge of her eyes. "And who decides who pays that price? You?"

Harper stepped closer, her eyes blazing. "Someone has to," she said. "Someone has to carry the burden of progress. Somehow I got involved."

Morgan stared at her, a mix of fear and disgust swirling in her chest. "Did you kill these people? If so you're nothing more than a monster," she said. "Just like any other killer."

Harper's expression softened, a hint of sadness flickering in her eyes. "Perhaps," she said. "But monsters are made, not born Miss Morgan."

The tension was shattered by a sudden blaring alarm. Red lights flashed in the corners of the room, and the device on the table began to hum.

Harper's eyes widened, and she spun toward the device. "What have you done?"

Morgan backed away, her heart racing. "What do you mean? I didn't do anything!"

Harper grabbed a remote from the table and pressed a button, but the alarm continued to blare. The device sparked, the wires writhing like snakes.

"We need to leave," Harper said, her voice tight with urgency.

Morgan hesitated, torn between fear and the need to grab as much evidence as she could. She darted to the shelves, grabbing a handful of binders and shoving them into her bag.

"Morgan, now!" Harper shouted.

The hum of the device grew louder, a high-pitched whine that made Morgan's ears ring. She bolted for the door, her bag slung over her shoulder. Harper followed close behind, slamming the door shut just as the device emitted a deafening roar of noise the origin of which was hard to place. The hallway shook, dust raining down from the ceiling. Harper leaned against the wall, her breathing ragged.

"You have no idea what you've done... what we've unleashed," she said, her voice trembling.

Morgan stared at her, her own breath coming in shallow gasps. "Maybe not," she said. "But I'm gonna to make sure everyone else does."

Harper's eyes darkened, her composure returning like a mask slipping into place. "You think you've

won?" she said. "This isn't a game and it's not over, Morgan. It's just beginning."

The young ghostwriter tightened her grip on her bag, the stolen binders pressing against her side. "I'll be ready," she said. "People just want the truth. And I think that's what you want too."

And with that, she turned and walked away, leaving Harper to face whatever was to come. Her protests that whatever this was would lead to the ruins of her empire seemed overstated and disingenuous. As she returned to her room and got behind a locked door she wondered... what was the deal in the basement... or was it a dungeon?

# CHAPTER 9

## The Betrayal

The rain hadn't let up in three days, drumming incessantly against the windows of Morgan's apartment in the city. It was a relentless, suffocating sound, much like the thoughts racing through her head. Stacks of papers, binders, and photographs from the estate were strewn across her coffee table and the floor, creating a chaotic mosaic of Harper's secrets. Morgan sat hunched over the table, flipping through a folder for the hundredth time, her eyes scanning the text as if the truth would suddenly leap off the page. She was finding info on poisons and a lot more. But it was like chasing a shadow—every revelation only seemed to deepened the mystery.

Her phone buzzed, startling her. She glanced at the screen: *Ethan.*

A knot tightened in her stomach. Ethan Cole had been her lifeline since she'd first uncovered Harper's tangled web of lies. A fellow writer he was smart, resourceful, and fiercely loyal—a friend she could count on when everything else felt uncertain. He had also been thru a legal ordeal and was well familiar with...death. However something about his recent behavior had set her on edge. His questions had grown sharper, his tone more insistent. He'd been pressing her for details about the evidence she'd collected, and while she'd chalked it up to genuine concern, a small voice in the back of her mind whispered about something darker.

Morgan ignored the call, letting it go to voicemail. She couldn't deal with Ethan right now. Not until she made sense of what she'd found.

She flipped to a photograph of Matthew Grayson, the investigative journalist who had vanished after probing too deeply into something in Harper's world. His face stared back at her, his eyes filled with a determination she recognized all too well.

"Why did she silence you?" Morgan muttered to herself. "What did you know that she couldn't risk you knowing?"

A knock at the door snapped her out of her thoughts. She froze, her heart pounding. It was nearly midnight—too late for casual visitors. And she wasn't expecting anyone.

Slowly, she rose from the couch and moved toward the door.

"Who is it?" she called, her voice steady despite the panic clawing at her chest.

"It's me," Ethan Cole's voice came from the other side. "Morgan, open up. We need to talk." He was a fellow author that had served 10 years in prison before being pardoned in the case where he had poisoned a brutal critic named Calvin Reese, over his book 'Blood on the Page'. While she didn't really know him well she considered him a good friend. Morgan hesitated at the door, her hand hovering over the lock. Something about his tone didn't sit well with her.

"Ethan, what's so urgent it couldn't wait until morning?" she asked, stalling for time and looking through the door's peep hole.

There was a pause, just long enough to raise her suspicion. "It's about Harper," Cole said. "I've got something you need to see. Please, Morgan. It's important."

She glanced back at the mess of documents on her table, her mind racing. If Cole had found something, she needed to know. But if her instincts were right, opening that door could be a mistake she might recover from. He might be unbalanced.

Grabbing the small .22 pistol she kept in the kitchen, Morgan slipped it into her housecoat pocket before unlocking the door.

Cole stood in the hallway, his dark coat soaked from the rain. It was awhile since she had seen him and his face was pale, his eyes shadowed with something she couldn't quite place. Guilt? Fear?

"My god, what is it at midnight on a Thursday?" she asked, keeping her voice calm. At least trying to.

Cole stepped inside, shaking off the rain. He scanned the room, his look lingering on the evidence spread across the tables of her apartment.

"You've been busy," he said, his tone light but his expression tense.

"I guess it comes with the territory," Morgan replied, crossing her arms. "What do you have for me?"

Cole hesitated, then reached into his coat pocket and pulled out a USB flash drive. "A while ago, about 6 years on a different project I found this in one of Harper's storage units," he said. "I think it's what Grayson was looking for before he disappeared."

Morgan's pulse quickened. "What's on it?"

"Proof," Ethan said. "Proof of everything Harper's been hiding. Names, dates, transactions—it's all there. Ya know I think she's killed people…"

Morgan took the flash drive, her fingers trembling. "Goddamn it! Why didn't you tell me about all this sooner? I was out at the estate and could have been in danger. Is she as freakin crazy as I think she is?"

"The short answer is yes!" Cole sighed, running a hand through his damp hair. "I didn't say anything because I didn't know who I could trust," he said. "Harper has eyes everywhere. The entire estate is wired with hidden cameras and microphones. For all I knew, you could have been working with her."

Morgan bristled. "Hell I still don't know what she's done or at least what we can prove. You think I'm helping her? I was just hired to write a book."

"I don't think that now," Cole said quickly. "But you can't blame me for being cautious. Harper doesn't play fair, Claire. You're gonna know that better than anyone when this is all over."

She nodded, though her unease hadn't subsided. "I need to see what's on this," she said, moving toward her laptop. The flash drive was old, its casing scratched and dented. Morgan plugged it in her computer, her screen coming to life with a series of encrypted files frowning she clicked on the first one.

A password prompt appeared.

"It's locked," she said, glancing at Cole.

He reached into his pocket and pulled out a scrap of paper. "Try this," he said, handing it to her.

Morgan typed in the password, and the screen flickered before displaying a list of folders. She opened the first one, her breath quickening as images and documents filled the screen.

Photographs of people—some she recognized from Harper's hidden room, others she didn't. Detailed dossiers with names, addresses, and disturbing notes about their "treatment" under Harper's project. Financial records tracing funds to offshore accounts.

"Is this what I think it is?" Morgan whispered, her eyes wide. "Did she and that damn machine in the basement kill these people?"

Cole nodded slowly, his expression remaining guarded and grave.

Morgan glanced at him. "Why do you look like someone just died?"

"Because they probably did!" he chuckled.

"Then this is everything we need to expose her This is what we've been waiting for," she said.

Cole shifted uncomfortably. "It's not that simple. There's more," he said. "Keep looking."

She opened another folder marked CM and her heart stopped.

There, among the files, was a photo of her.

Her name was typed in bold letters above a detailed surveillance report. It listed her address, her habits, and even her movements over the past months before she went to the estate. But it was the final section that chilled her to the bone: "Subject identified as a potential risk. Contingency plan in place."

"What the hell is this?" Morgan demanded, her voice shaking.

Cole didn't answer.

The silence between them stretched, growing heavier with each passing moment. Morgan turned to face Ethan, her hand instinctively moving to her pocket where the gun rested.

"You knew," she said, her voice barely above a whisper.

Cole's jaw tightened. "I didn't know until day before yesterday," he said. "Morgan... I now think she's had her eye on you from the beginning."

"And you didn't think to tell me?" Morgan snapped.

"I was trying to protect you," Cole said, stepping closer. "I didn't want to scare you off before we could get enough evidence to take her down. And you were so excited about the new project and the money..."

Morgan shook her head, backing away. "You're lying. You've been lying to me this whole time, haven't you?"

Cole's eyes flickered with something she couldn't place—regret, maybe, or something darker. "It's not what you think," he said. "I was working with her at first, yes, but only because I didn't have a choice. She's got leverage on me, Morgan. And here's a newsflash...she has leverage on everyone."

Morgan's stomach churned. "You've been feeding her information," she said, the realization hitting her like a blow. "That's how she's stayed one step ahead of me."

Cole didn't deny it and sat there in silence.

Morgan's hand tightened around the gun in her pocket. "Why are you here, Ethan? What's your real reason for coming tonight at 1 in the damn morning?"

Cole hesitated, his face a mask of conflict. "I came to warn you," he said finally. "Harper knows you have taken some info and she now thinks you can't be trusted. And don't look now but she's sending someone to 'clean up the mess'. I think you really need to get the hell outta here!" he said.

Morgan stared at him, her mind racing. Could she trust him? Or was this just another layer of the game Harper was playing?

"How do I know you're not the one she sent?" she asked, her voice trembling.

Cole's face fell, and for the first time, he looked genuinely hurt. "Morgan, I've made mistakes," he said. "But I'm not here to hurt you. I'm your friend and I am trying to make this right."

Before she could respond, a loud crash echoed from the hallway outside.

Morgan's heart leapt into her throat. Ethan's head snapped toward the door, his hand moving to the gun holstered under his coat.

"They're here," he said, his voice tense.

"Who?" Morgan demanded, her fear mounting.

Cole grabbed her arm, pulling her toward the window. "No time to explain," he said. "We need to move… now!"

The sound of a few sets of heavy footsteps grew louder, accompanied by the muffled voices of men barking orders at a whisper.

Morgan yanked her arm free, her mind racing. "I'm not going anywhere until you tell me what's going on," she said.

Cole glared at her. "If we stay here, you'll die," he said. "Is that what you want?"

The door burst open before Morgan could respond. Two men in dark suits stormed in, their faces obscured by balaclavas.

Cole didn't hesitate. He drew his gun and fired, the sharp crack of the shot ringing in Morgan's ears. One of the men dropped, but the other lunged at Ethan, tackling him to the ground.

Morgan stumbled back, pulling out her gun her with heart pounding as the room descended into chaos. Cole and the man grappled on the floor, the gun skidding across the hardwood.

"Run!" Cole shouted to her, his voice strained.

Morgan didn't need to be told twice. She grabbed the flash drive and bolted for the fire escape, her legs trembling as she climbed out into the stormy night. The rain hit her like icy needles, soaking her to the bone in seconds as she descended the metal stairs. Behind her, she heard the sound of a struggle, some yelling followed by a few more gunshots.

She didn't look back.

Morgan hit the ground running, clutching the flash drive like a lifeline. The city blurred around her, the rain obscuring everything but the pounding of her heart and the certainty that she couldn't stop. Not now. Not ever. Cole's possible betrayal had cut deep, but it had also ignited something within her. Harper had underestimated her. And if she was as evil as Cole and the intel indicated, Morgan was going to help make her pay for her sins.

# CHAPTER 10

## A Journal's Truth

The journal sat on the desk like a coiled snake, waiting to strike. Its leather cover was cracked and worn, the edges frayed from decades of use. Morgan stared at it, her pulse quickening. She had spent weeks chasing Harper's secrets, piecing together the fragments of a story that refused to be told. This journal—this relic found hidden beneath a false panel in Harper's mahogany desk—was possibly the final missing piece. At this point it was very obvious that this was not going to be a typical feel good memoir. Her fingers hovered over the clasp, trembling slightly. She took a deep breath, steadying herself. For weeks, Morgan had imagined this moment. She had envisioned triumph, the satisfaction of uncovering the truth. But now, with the journal open and just inches away, she felt something entirely different: complete dread.

She had made herself scarce and few days later she was back home. The air in her 6th floor apartment was heavy and now thick with the smell of old wood and leather. Outside, the storm raged, rain hammering against the windows in an erratic rhythm. It was as if the world itself knew what she was about to uncover and wanted to warn her against it. She reached for the clasp and flicked it open. The strap fell away with a quiet snap. Morgan hesitated for a moment longer, then opened the journal to the first page.nThe handwriting was elegant but rushed, the ink faded in places. April 12, 1987. The date was scrawled at the top, followed by a single line that sent a chill down her spine:

*"They said it would work, but I'm not sure I believe them."*

Her eyes darted across the page. The entry was brief, cryptic, the words trailing off as if Harper had been too afraid to commit her thoughts to paper. She turned the page, her heartbeat loud in her ears. The early entries were mundane, almost banal: musings about Harper's writing, frustrations with the publishing industry, and notes for potential book ideas. But as Morgan read on, the tone began to shift. The language grew darker, the sentences more fractured.

*"May 3, 1987. The first subject has arrived. I thought it would be exciting, but it's terrifying. The equipment hums like a living thing, and the room feels colder than it should. Dr. Calloway says it's normal, but what does he know about normal?"*

Morgan thought… Dr. Calloway? She had seen his name before, buried in one of the articles she'd found. He was a disgraced neuroscientist linked to a series of controversial experiments in the late 1970s involving manipulations of the brain via surgical intervention. She had suspected Harper was involved with him, but now this journal confirmed it.

She turned the page, her stomach tied in knots.

*"June 15, 1987. Subject 002 didn't make it. The procedure was too much for her. Calloway insists we're making progress, but I can't get her face out of my mind. She was just a girl, barely out of college. I keep telling myself it's for the greater good, but I'm starting to wonder if that's just another lie."*

She closed her eyes, nausea rising in her throat. Harper had always presented herself as a literary genius, a visionary who lived for her craft. But this… this was something else entirely. It appeared that they were doing experiments that rivaled that of the Nazi's in WW2! She opened her eyes and kept reading, driven by a morbid curiosity she couldn't suppress. The entries grew more erratic, the writing sloppier as if Harper had been unraveling.

*"July 22, 1987. Calloway says we're ready for a larger trial, but I'm not convinced. The memory implants are unstable, and the erasures are leaving gaps we can't explain. The subjects are starting to notice. One of them—Subject 004—keeps talking about shadows in her dreams. It's probably nothing, but it IS unsettling. "* It said.

Shivering with the words sinking into her skin like ice water she wondered what had they done to these people? At this point all she knew for sure was that they were dead.

She flipped through the pages, skimming the entries until she reached one that made her freeze. The date was circled in red ink:

*"September 11, 1987.*
*Matthew showed up today. I told him it wasn't a good time, but he insisted. He knows too much, and I can't risk him exposing us. Calloway says we should 'handle' him, but I don't have the stomach for that. Maybe if I can convince him to leave it alone so we can avoid... drastic measures."*

Matthew. The investigative journalist who had disappeared under mysterious circumstances. The man whose name had haunted Morgan since she first stumbled upon Harper's documents. Her hands trembled as she turned the page. The next entry was shorter, the handwriting jagged and uneven:

*"September 8, 1987. It's done. Matthew won't be a problem anymore. I told myself it was for the best, but I can't stop shaking. He was my friend damn it! How did I let it come to this?"*

Morgan's vision blurred as tears filled her eyes. Matthew hadn't just disappeared, Harper had orchestrated his death! She slammed the journal shut, her pulse more rapid. The truth was overwhelming, a tidal wave of horror and betrayal. Harper wasn't just a celebrated author she was manipulative genius—she was a monster.

Morgan shoved the journal into her bag, her mind racing. This was the evidence she needed to expose Harper to finally bring her down. But the weight of what she'd uncovered made her knees weak. And who would believe her? And she couldn't turn to Cole for help as he was a convicted felon who had killed a critic.

The sound of footsteps in the hallway jolted her out of her thoughts. She froze, her heart pounding.

"Morgan?" a voice called softly.

Her stomach twisted. It was Cole!

She hadn't seen him in days—not since she'd discovered his connection to Harper . She didn't know if he was here to help her or to silence her.

The footsteps stopped outside the door. "Morgan, I know you're in there," Cole said. "Open up. We need to talk."

She stood motionless, her mind racing. The storm outside roared, the thunder masking the sound of her breathing.

"Harper knows," Cole said through the door his voice urgent. "She knows what you've found. You're not safe here!"

Morgan hesitated, her hand instinctively reaching for the small gun still in her pocket. Finally, she took the chain off and opened the door

"What are you doing here?" she demanded, her voice steady despite the fear coursing through her veins.

Cole's face was pale, his eyes darting nervously toward the hallway. "I came to warn you," he said. " Harper's people are on their way again. If they find you, they won't hesitate and I believe they will kill you."

Morgan narrowed her eyes. "How do I know you're not one of them?"

Cole held up his hands. "I get it. You don't trust me. Fine. But let's be real, if I wanted you dead, you wouldn't be standing here right now."

Her grip on the gun tightened, but before she could respond, the sound of a car pulling up outside made her blood run cold.

Cole glanced toward the window. "We need to move," he said, his voice low. "Now."

The next few minutes were a blur. The power went out. Cole, his movements quick and deliberate, led her though the darkness. Day 5 of the storms outside had turned the city into a swirling chaos of flooding, wind and rain. The sound was almost deafening as

they slipped out through a back door. They ran toward Cole's car, a Mustang parked just beyond the gate. He yanked open the driver's side door and gestured for her to get in.

Morgan hesitated, her instincts screaming at her to run in the opposite direction. But the sight of headlights in the rain approaching in the distance forced her to make a decision. She climbed into the car, slamming the door behind her. Cole started the engine, the tires skidding on the wet pavement as they sped away. The ride was silent, tension crackling between them like static electricity. Morgan clutched her bag, her thoughts a chaotic swirl of fear and anger.

"Where are we going?" she asked finally.

"Someplace safe, someplace secure" Cole said, his voice tight.

Morgan didn't believe him, but she had no other options. For now, she would have to play along. And besides she still had the gun in her pocket, if it came to that.

As the car sped through the rain-soaked streets, Morgan stared out the window, her reflection staring back at her. The journal in her bag felt like a ticking bomb, its unknown secrets threatening to destroy everything Harper had built—and possibly everyone who got in her way including a young, eager, writer. But one thing was super clear: Morgan was not backing down. Harper had spent decades hiding the truth. Painful as it was she had decided to void the contract and do the book on her own. Harper will be furious and will take this to court. she thought. She didn't care. Now, Morgan was going to make sure the world finally knew the full story of the legendary suspense author. She felt it was the least she could do. The fact of the matter was she now knew that Vivian Harper was not a very nice person. The thought crossed her mind that the famous author's books about murder were not fiction after all!

# CHAPTER 11

## The Final Chapter?

The storm had calmed by the time Morgan arrived back at the mansion. The night air was damp, the scent of wet earth and decaying leaves hanging heavily. She sat outside the gat4e for what seemed like an hour, As she parked her car under a flickering streetlight, she glanced up at the looming silhouette of the mansion. Its windows, dark and hollow, gave it the look of a forgotten place, abandoned and untouched for years. But from her previous stay Morgan knew better. She knew this place wasn't abandoned—it was a vault for secrets, a trap set by the owner. Harper was out of the country in Europe getting an award for her latest novel. She'd be gone for 3 weeks.

For a moment, she sat in the car, staring at the house, weighing her options. She'd come too far to turn back now, but the weight of what she was carrying—the journal—felt heavier than ever. But if she was going to go to the FBI she needed more. The answers she sought, the truth she needed, were contained within those walls and in those fragile pages. It was more than just a record of Harper's dark past. The journal was a key, and Morgan had no idea what doors it would open, or what horrors awaited behind them. And she kept coming back to the machine in the dungeon. Finally, she grabbed the journal from the passenger seat and tucked it under her arm. She could feel the cool leather of its cover against her skin, like the pulse of something alive. It was a strange sensation, almost as if the journal itself was holding its breath, waiting for her to unlock its truth.

The mansion stood silently the hill, and with a deep breath, Morgan exited the car and walked toward the front door. Her boots crunched against the gravel as she made her way up to the building. The air seemed to grow colder with every step, an unsettling chill settling deep into her bones. She reached the steps of the porch and paused for a moment, her hand hovering over the brass doorknob. This was it!

Her fingers tightened around the knob, and she twisted it. Surprisingly the huge door creaked open, revealing the darkness inside. The smell of mildew and old wood again greeted her as she stepped across the threshold. The dark foyer and massive staircase felt strangely alive, as if the mansion itself was watching her, waiting for her next move.

Morgan swallowed hard and took a cautious step forward. Her every instinct screamed at her to turn around, to run far away from this place. But she knew she couldn't leave—not now, not when she was so close to the truth. She also realized that she was probably under surveillance and that Harper's staff had to still be on the estate somewhere. She was still surprised that the front door had been left unlocked. As she looked around the faint hum of the mansion's electrical system buzzed in the background, barely audible beneath the pounding of

Morgan's heart. She took a few more steps, moving slowly toward the staircase that would take her to the second floor, to the study. Harper's study.

Her phone buzzed in her pocket, the vibration jarring in the stillness of the mansion. Morgan jumped, startled by the interruption. She pulled the phone out, seeing Ethan's name flashing on the screen.

Her finger hovered over the green button. She should pick up. She knew that. But there was something in Ethan Cole's voice the last time they spoke that had left her unsettled, something she couldn't shake.

Still, she pressed the button. "Ethan?"

"Where are you?" his voice was tight and urgent.

"I'm there," she said softly, glancing around the darkened room. The walls seemed to close in on her as she spoke.

"Morgan, listen to me," Cole said, his voice strained. "You need to leave. Now. Harper knows. Even from across the Atlantic he knows you're in there! If you don't leave now, you're walking into a trap. This place—she's got people there. Dangerous people."

"I'm not leaving," Morgan replied, her voice steady despite the fear bubbling up in her gut. "I came for the truth, and I'm going to find it. You can't stop me and neither can she!"

There was a long pause on the other end of the line. Morgan could hear Cole's breathing, sharp and heavy, as though he was wrestling with something. Finally, he spoke again, his tone softer.

"Morgan, please. You don't know what you're dealing with. Harper —she's not the person you think she is. You need to trust me. Just get out of there. I can help you."

But Morgan couldn't trust him. Not now. Not after everything she'd discovered. "I have to do this," she said, her voice firm.

Cole let out a frustrated sigh. "Fine. I got your back. But please don't say I didn't warn you."

Before she could respond, he had hung up.

The silence that followed was deafening. Morgan shoved the phone back into her pocket and exhaled deeply. Her hand went instinctively to the small weapon tucked into the waistband of her jeans. It was an old habit, one that comforted her more than she liked to admit. With the storm outside and the palpable tension in the house, the gun felt like the only thing standing between her and whatever Harper had planned.

Moving with caution she made her way up the stairs, each step creaking under her weight. Harper's study,

the one with the weird flying monkey and huge portrait was at the end of the hall. As Morgan approached the huge door, she could feel her pulse quickening. This was it. The moment she'd been building up to. She had to get inside. The journal, different from the one she had already taken— Harper's new journal—was her only leverage. Morgan took a deep breath and pushed open the door.

She turned on the light. Harper sat behind her desk, her sharp eyes immediately locking onto Morgan. Her expression was unreadable, her lips pressed into a thin line, her posture was stiff and she appears to be calm, controlled. As if she had been expecting Morgan all along.

"So," Harper said coolly, "you've come to finish what you started, eh?."

Morgan stepped into the room, her heart pounding. She couldn't back down now. She couldn't let Harper take this from her. She had to confront the truth, even if it meant facing the woman who had spent years hiding behind lies and manipulation.

Morgan her voice unwavering, "I thought you were in Europe getting an award for your book."

"I'm not," she said. After pausing she continued. "You know I could shoot and kill you right now as an intruder."

"I just came for the truth," Morgan said.

Harper's lips curled into a faint, almost pitying smile. "The truth," she repeated. "You think you want the truth. But I've lived through things you can't even imagine. You have no idea what you're asking for, Morgan."

Morgan felt the weight of Harper's eyes as they seemed to bore into her. Every instinct told her to run, but she held her ground. "I know exactly what you've done. And I know you're trying to bury it. But it won't work anymore. I have the journal!"

At the mention of the journal, Harper's smile faded, and for a fleeting moment, Morgan saw something akin to fear in her eyes. But it was gone in an instant, replaced by the calm, composed façade Morgan had come to expect.

"I see," Harper said, her voice icy. "You think that journal changes anything? You're wrong. That book is just a tool, a means to an end. If you think exposing me will destroy everything I've built, then you're as naive as you look."

"I don't need to destroy you," Morgan said, stepping forward. "I just need to make sure the truth is known. The world needs to know what you've done. So you can forget about the memoir. I am writing my own book now,"

Harper's eyes narrowed, and she stood from behind her desk. "Good luck with that!" She said. Her tall, slender figure was imposing, but Morgan stood firm. She wouldn't back down. Not now.

"You think you can just waltz in here and take my power from me?" Harper sneered. "I've spent decades building something far greater than you can comprehend. You're just a pawn in my game, sweetie. And you'll regret ever trying to cross me. Be a good girl, finish the project, take the money and move on."

Morgan's stomach twisted, but she didn't flinch. "You've hurt too many people. This ends tonight."

Harper's expression hardened. "You're playing a dangerous game, Morgan. But I've played it far longer than you."

Without warning, Harper reached into the drawer of her desk and pulled out a .357 revolver. The metallic gleam and largeness of her weapon was almost too much to bear. Morgan's heart skipped a beat as she instinctively took a step back and pulled out her own weapon.

Harper laughed out loud. "What are you gonna do with that little thing? Put it down," she commanded, her voice low and controlled.

Morgan froze. Her hand twitched, but she didn't lower the .22. She couldn't.

"You won't kill me," Morgan said, her voice shaking but defiant. "Not like this."

Harper's lips twisted into a cruel smile. "You're right. I don't need to kill you. Not yet. But I could…"

The silence between them grew thick. Morgan could feel the weight of the gun in Harper's hand, the tension hanging in the air just like a loaded weapon. The storm outside had quieted, but inside, the world felt like it was teetering on the edge of destruction.

"Put it down, Morgan," Harper said again, her voice softer this time. "You don't want to make this any worse than it already is. Let's work this out."

Morgan's breath quickened. Her fingers tightened around the gun, but she knew she couldn't win this fight. Not with a gun like that and not with Harper in control.

As the minutes stretched on, her mind began to race. The journal. The truth. She couldn't let it slip away. The answer, the way forward, was right in front of her.

Before Harper could react, Morgan lunged for the journal, knocking it from the desk with a force that startled them both. The pages spilled out onto the floor, a flood of words, and Morgan's heart raced as she scrambled to gather them.

Each page was a piece of Harper's twisted legacy, each sentence a testament to the darkness the woman had buried beneath layers of lies. Harper made a move to stop her, but Morgan was faster. She grabbed the journal, clutching it to her chest. The moment of silence that followed felt like an eternity. Then, the door slammed open, and the sound of footsteps echoed from the hallway. Morgan's heart stopped.

Harper's smile was cold. "You should have left when you had the chance, Morgan. Now, you're mine."

Suddenly the power went out again and Morgan sliping behind the heavy curtains and thru the darkness somehow found her way out of the mansion to her car and back to the city. During the trip Harper had called her several times.

# CHAPTER 12

## The Aftermath

The light of the early morning sun cut through the dusty blinds, creating strips of golden light that seemed to slice through the fog in Morgan's mind. She stared down at the journal in her lap. She had slept with it and her gun. Her fingers ran across the worn leather cover, as though trying to memorize its texture, as if it could give her some kind of guidance, a way out of the maze she had found herself in. The pages inside contained truths that, once revealed, had irreversibly altered the course of her life.

Harper's empire of lies and manipulation was over, and with it, the illusion Morgan had built around her idol—Harper's illusion of control, of certainty, of righteousness. The revelations had been explosive, shocking enough to shake even the most hardened investigators, yet it had come at a cost. The constant threat from Harper's lawyers were a source of concern but Morgan's publisher assured her they were on solid legal ground and that the FBI and State Police were on top the case.

To Morgan giving up the money was hard but she felt she had achieved what she set out to do. The FBI arrested Harper and she was now in custody. The charges included attempted murder, illegal disposal of a human body and a wide variety of other charges going back to 1963. With her new book Morgan would see to it that the world knew the dark truth behind the glamorous, dangerous author Morgan had once admired.

But Morgan didn't feel victorious. The weight of the journal, once a symbol of her determination, now felt like a reminder of everything she had lost in the process of pursuing that elusive truth. The grizzly details of Doctor Cooperman's brain operations in the dungeon of the mansion would haunt her for years. The phone buzzed again, breaking the silence in the room. She'd been dreading this. The name on the screen was enough to freeze her in place. 'Ethan'.

Her heart thudded painfully against her ribs, the connection between them still unresolved, the fragile thread of trust stretched thin. She had ignored his calls the night before, unwilling to hear his disappointment or his warnings. Now, the screen blinked up at her with the weight of unspoken things. She could ignore it. But she knew she couldn't avoid this forever. It was time to face him. Time to face the consequences of her decisions.

She answered the call, her thumb shaking just slightly as she swiped the screen.

"Morgan," Cole's voice came through, low and heavy. There was a tiredness to it, a depth of frustration that made her stomach tighten. "We need to talk. I am worried about your safety."

"I know," Morgan whispered, her voice hoarse, as if the words had been lodged in her throat for days.

There was a long pause on the other end, as though Ethan were gathering his thoughts before speaking again. When he did, his tone was softer but insistent.

"You exposed Harper's crimes, Morgan. You did the right thing. But now… now, you need to think about what happens next. What you're going to do with all of this. The truth—it's not going to fix everything or anything really. You can't undo what's been done."

"I know," she said again, her voice trembling this time. "I thought it would… I thought it would fix… me. That bringing everything into the light would somehow make it all better. But it doesn't. It's not enough. All those people are still… dead."

Cole sighed, the sound of it carrying an overwhelming sense of exhaustion. "The truth doesn't heal wounds, Morgan. It opens them. You've got to confront that now. You've done the hard part. But don't let it destroy you. Besides the FBI has the ball now. If they charge her they charge her."

Morgan closed her eyes. The guilt had been gnawing at her for so long. She had sacrificed so much in the name of exposing Harper. There was also the legal matter If the signed NDA and Harper's attorney's wanted a return of the deposit Morgan had been paid and now wanted to block any book related to Vivian Harper. The project had come at a high cost for writer Claire Morgan. She had ignored the people who cared about her, shut them out in her quest for justice and accomplishment. Ethan Cole had tried to warn her, but she hadn't listened. She hadn't known

131

how to listen to anything but her own desperate need to succeed both as a writer and as a woman.

"I don't know how to fix this, Ethan," she said, her voice breaking. "I don't know how to fix... me."

Another long silence passed between them before Cole responded. "You don't have to fix anything. You just have to stop running from it. Stop running from it. It's gonna be an awesome book!"

Morgan swallowed hard, her chest tight. "I don't think I can face this alone."

"You don't have to," Cole said quietly. "I'm here. I'm not going anywhere. But you've got to take that first step. You've already done the hardest thing— you brought the truth to light and you've got a great first draft.. You've done the research. Now it's time to make peace with it and write a best seller!"

The café was small, tucked into a quiet corner of the city, the type of place where the world seemed to slow down. The soft hum of conversation, the clinking of coffee cups, the warmth of the room—everything felt like a brief reprieve from the chaos of the world outside. Morgan had suggested the café, knowing that neither of them could face another heavy talk in her cramped apartment.

When she arrived, Ethan Cole was already seated at a corner table, his hands wrapped around a coffee cup. His face was tired, worn, like a man who had spent too many sleepless nights running on nothing but adrenaline. His dark eyes caught hers as soon as she entered, and Morgan saw the same sorrow there that she had been carrying with her.

As she sat down, the space between them felt enormous. No words were spoken for a few moments. Neither of them knew where to begin. It had been too long since they'd last been in the same room, and the events of the past few weeks had made everything so much more complicated. But Morgan knew she couldn't move forward without this conversation. She couldn't carry the weight of everything on her own anymore.

"I'm sorry," she said finally, her voice cracking slightly. "I should've listened… you warned me."

Cole didn't answer right away, but his gaze softened. His eyes seemed to say everything without words. He understood. She had been consumed by the need to expose the truth, to right the wrongs Harper had committed, and in doing so, write a top notch best seller. But Morgan realized that she had lost sight of the people who mattered most to her. And that included Cole. When he was in prison for killing Book Reviewer Calvin Reese over his book 'Death on the Page', Morgan is one of only a handful of people that visited him behind bars.

"I don't blame you for going after Harper," Cole said after a long pause. "You were right to expose her. But you didn't stop to think about what it would cost you. What it would cost us?"

"I was trying to fix something," Morgan whispered, almost to herself. "I thought that if I could just bring the truth to light, everything would be better. That I could finally fix all the things I've done, all the mistakes I've made."

"Truth doesn't work like that," Ethan replied. "It doesn't heal wounds—it exposes them. It forces us to face what we've been hiding from. It's hard. It's painful. But you can't keep running from it."

Morgan let his words sink in. She had been running—running from the consequences of her actions, from the guilt of taking down one of her hereos. It was following

134

her like a shadow. She thought that exposing Harper's darkness would bring clarity, but in truth, it had only uncovered more of her own darkness. Her hands tightened around the journal, the pages within still holding secrets, but now, those secrets were not just Harper's. They were hers too.

"I didn't know how to stop," Morgan admitted, her voice small. "I was so consumed by what Harper had done and the prospect of success and money that I couldn't see what I was doing to myself. To us."

Cole's expression softened. "You don't have to do this alone, Morgan. We can work through this together. But you need to forgive yourself. That's the only way to move forward. All in all it's really not that bad."

Morgan let out a shaky breath, her heart heavy in her chest. "How do I forgive myself, Ethan? How do I live with the things I now know?"

"You start by accepting them," Ethan said quietly. "You can't undo the past, Morgan. But you can choose how to move forward. You don't need to fix everything—you just need to stop trying to outrun it. The truth is messy, and it doesn't come with a neat bow on top. Write the book, it's a start. And sometimes, that's enough."

Claire met Ethan's eyes, her heart swelling with something she hadn't felt in a long time—hope. It was a fragile thing, like a flickering light, but it was there, just enough to make her believe that maybe, just maybe, she could begin to make peace with herself, write the novel and make a little money.

"You're right," she said, her voice steadier now. "I can't undo what's been done. But I can stop running from it. I can stop trying to fix it all by myself."

Ethan reached across the table, his hand brushing against hers. "You don't have to do it alone. I'm here." And she now realized he was sweet on her.

The days that followed were a blur of media frenzy, legal proceedings, and endless questions. Harper's arrest was the subject of headlines for weeks, and the world seemed to revel in the exposure of her crimes. Morgan watched from the sidelines, feeling the weight of the chaos she had set in motion. The investigation into Harper's activities was just beginning, and the authorities were piecing together the extent of her empire. But as the world turned its attention to Harper, Morgan also felt the sharp sting of the legal consequences of her actions.

But something had changed in Morgan. The guilt was unnecessary and unjustified. It had once consumed her but now felt more like a distant echo, one that she was learning to live with rather than be controlled by. It wasn't gone, not entirely, but she had begun to accept it, to accept herself. She wasn't perfect. She had made mistakes—some big ones—but she had also taken responsibility. She had done what she thought was right, even if it had cost her. And the book was gonna be stellar. And so slowly, she began to believe that maybe, just maybe, she could move on.

Ethan had been there for her every step of the way, offering support without judgment, editing help with her various writing projects and giving her space when she needed it, but never leaving her alone in the dark. With him by her side, Morgan felt like she could face whatever came next.

In the end, Morgan knew that peace and success wasn't something that could be granted or given to her by anyone else. It was something she had to find within herself and produce with her works. And though the road ahead was still uncertain, she knew she had taken the first strong steps. She no longer felt lost in the aftermath of her actions. Instead, she was starting to see the possibility of a future that didn't revolve around guilt and regret. It wasn't a perfect peace—she knew it would take time—but it was hers to build now. And she had the tools to do it.

The following weeks brought the closure Morgan hadn't known she needed. The media frenzy surrounding Harper's arrest eventually died down, replaced by the next big scandal. And there was significant interest in her new book. But for Morgan, it wasn't just about the headlines anymore—it was about the silence that had settled in her heart. For the first time in a long time, she could breathe without the constant pressure of Harper hanging over her.

As the investigation into Harper's criminal action continued, Morgan found herself involved in the process. Once Harper was arrested Morgan worked with the authorities, providing her insight into Harper's operations and helping to piece together the final aspects of the story that would bring her down. But there was a bittersweet realization as the pieces fell into place. Harper's grand façade, which had once captivated Morgan, now seemed like nothing more than a hollow shell. The woman she had once admired was nothing but a figment of her own past and her imagination.

In addition to being a accomplice of Doctor Cooperman's horrific brain experiments which resulted in at least 5 deaths Harper had amassed a huge volume of files on virtually everyone from celebrities to politicians to business men and women and then used that information to blackmail and influence people to do exactly what she wanted. She is charged with 13 felony counts that could end with her in prison for life.

But the hardest part wasn't about Harper anymore. It was about Morgan coming to terms with her own complicity in the story. She had allowed herself to be manipulated. She had let her ambition allow her to make dumb choices that led her down this dark path. And yet, somehow, she had survived. And as the truth had come to light, so had Morgan's own redemption. The hardest thing was to accept that she was still worthy of redemption, no matter what.

One evening, several weeks after the dust had settled, Morgan sat in the quiet of her apartment, the journal now tucked safely away in the hands of the FBI. She had no more need for it—it had served its purpose. What remained now was a sense of finality. The truth had been uncovered. The investigation was wrapping up. And Morgan had a chance to rebuild her life with her new blockbuster book.

There was a soft knock at the door. It was a sound Morgan had come to expect at odd hours, especially after everything had happened—Ethan had often stopped by to check in on her. This time, however, it felt different. She knew this knock.

She opened the door to find Cole standing there, his familiar, comforting presence standing in the threshold. His expression was gentle, but there was something in his eyes that made Morgan's heart flutter. He wasn't here for business, or to discuss things, or to offer guidance. He was here for her. And for the first time in what felt like forever, Morgan felt like she didn't have to carry the burden alone anymore.

Ethan entered, the warm glow of the hallway light spilling across the room. He looked at Morgan for a moment, his gaze lingering before he spoke softly.

"I've been thinking," he said, his voice calm but sure. "You've done the hardest thing anyone could do. You've faced the truth, even when it cost you everything. But now it's time to ask yourself what you want. Who do you want to be now?"

Morgan looked at him, the weight of his question sinking in. For so long, she had been chasing after a solution—an answer to fix the wrongs of her past. She had sought justice, had sought the truth, but now she realized that the most important question wasn't about Harper or the crimes she had uncovered. It was about Morgan.

"What do I want?" she repeated, the words tasting foreign in her mouth. "I don't know if I've ever asked myself that."

Ethan smiled slightly, sitting down on the edge of the couch. He gestured for her to join him, and she did, sitting beside him in the stillness. The world outside had moved on, but here, in this small apartment, it felt like everything had stopped, as if it was just the two of them.

"You don't have to have all the answers right now," Ethan said gently. "But you have a choice, Morgan. You can either keep letting your past define you, or you can step into your future and start fresh. The world is wide open. What do you want to do with it?"

Claire let the question sit with her. She didn't need to make an immediate decision, but for the first time in what felt like an eternity, she realized that she wasn't bound to her mistakes. She wasn't defined by her association with Harper or by the guilt that had driven her to expose the truth. She had the power to choose. She could decide who she was going to be moving forward.

"I want to stop running," she said, her voice firm, but not without hesitation. "I want to live without the weight of my past decisions hanging over me. I want to be someone who doesn't have to fix everything. Just... someone who can breathe and make peace with what's happened."

Cole nodded, the smile that spread across his face warm and full of pride. "That's a good place to start."

They sat there together, the quiet surrounding them both, each lost in their own thoughts but sharing the weight of everything that had come before. In this space, there was no more guilt, no more shame—just two people who had walked through the fire and had somehow come out stronger.

In the months that followed, Morgan slowly began to rebuild her life. She took time to process everything that had happened, but she no longer felt like she was buried beneath the weight of it all. She moved forward in small, deliberate steps. She reconnected with old friends, started to rebuild relationships she had neglected in her single-minded pursuit of the truth. Most importantly, she took time for herself—time to heal, time to rediscover who she was without the shadow of the Harper project looming over her. And she found a publisher and poured herself into the new book.

Ethan remained by her side, the bond between them slowly re-strengthening. Though they had both been damaged by the events that had transpired, they were also healed, together. And as they moved forward, Morgan found herself more open to the possibilities ahead—no longer paralyzed by fear or guilt, but instead fueled by the hope of a future she could shape for herself.

She never forgot what had happened, but the weight of it became lighter as she learned to live with the consequences. She accepted that there would be no perfect resolution, no neat ending. There would always be the aftershocks of the choices she had made, the mistakes she had lived through. But now, those aftershocks didn't define her. They were just part of the story—part of the truth that had ultimately set her free.

And in the quiet moments, when she would sit with herself, Morgan knew that peace was not a place she would ever really arrive at—peace was a journey, one that she would continue to walk, step by step, for the rest of her life.

And for the first time, she was ready to take that journey. The final chapter in that story had been written. But Morgan's story was far from over.

# CHAPTER 13

## Consequences

The prisoner visiting room was dark, the only light coming from a solitary lamp overhead. Morgan sat across from Harper, the woman she had once admired, now a shell of the powerful figure she had once been. Just another convict. Her eyes were shadowed, her posture rigid, but beneath the veneer of defiance, Morgan could see cracks—so many cracks.

They had been through hell together, but this interview, this confrontation, this moment, was different. The truth had been exposed, and the weight of everything she had done—was now too much to ignore. It had been a long time coming, but now, as Morgan sat in the silence, her stomach churning with a strange combination of anger and understanding, she knew this was the final reckoning. She looked haggard and out of place in her county issued orange jumpsuit.

"Orange is the new black," she joked. Harper sat down in one of the metal chairs. She leaned forward, her gaze locking onto Morgan's. "You don't look like the triumphant hero the papers painted you out to be. But you're getting lots of good press for the book!"

Morgan didn't flinch. She had spent too long in this woman's shadow to let her words sting. She had learned that the power of words lay in their ability to control, but Morgan wouldn't let Harper control her anymore. Not after everything.

"Don't flatter me or yourself," Morgan replied, her voice steady. "I'm not a hero. I never was."

Harper's lips curled into a bitter smile. "You think you're the only one who's paying for their sins?" She leaned back in her chair, her fingers drumming on the table. "You think that exposing me is going to cleanse your soul? The damage you've done to yourself, Morgan... It's not something you can undo. Your not totally innocent you know," she said.

"I didn't do anything for me," Morgan shot back, her voice growing cold. "I did it because you've been lying to everyone including yourself. You built an empire on blood, lies, and manipulation. And I'm just making sure the world knows the truth, the whole truth and nothing but the truth... you should remember that sentence as you're gonna need it when you get to court," she smiled.

"That's not gonna happen. Besides... the truth?" Harper repeated, her tone like a bitter aftertaste. "You think truth is some magic cure? It's not. It doesn't fix things. It doesn't make you whole. All it does is strip you down to the core, leaving you with nothing but your own soul and rotting bones."

Morgan paused, looking at her, her fingers tightening around the edge of the chair. "I don't need to be whole anymore. I just need to know that what I did what was right. That's all I have left."

Harper let out a harsh laugh. "You want to feel righteous? Then why do you look so damn broken? You think you can walk away from this with your hands clean? With your conscience clear? Fat chance sweetheart!"

"I'm not walking away," Morgan said slowly. "I'm facing the consequences. Just like you. Just like we all have to. And I don't care if the book sells or not."

Harper's eyes narrowed. "Consequences…" she mused, her voice lowering into something more contemplative. "Tell me, Morgan, what happens when those consequences start to eat away at you? When every decision you've made, every lie you've told, every choice you've avoided… what happens then? Can you live with it?"

Part of her didn't know what she was talking about so Morgan swallowed hard. She had spent weeks, nay months, trying to convince herself she could deal with anything and that bringing Harper to justice would somehow free her from the weight of her own complicity. But in the quiet of this room, with Harper's gaze cutting through her like a knife, Morgan felt the truth of what Harper was saying. The consequences of their actions weren't just external—they festered deep inside your bones, twisting you until you couldn't escape.

"I don't know," Morgan admitted, her voice quieter now, tinged with uncertainty. "But I have to try."
"Try?" Harper repeated, her lips curling into a half-smirk. "You think it will be enough? Think trying to do the right thing will erase the evil you've done?"

Morgan's heart skipped. "What evil?" It was a question she had asked herself countless times in the aftermath of the exposure. Could she ever truly move on from what she had been a part of? She had thought that the truth— Harper's crimes, the secrets she uncovered—would somehow absolve her. But now she saw that truth was not a balm... but a blade.

"No," Morgan whispered. "I don't think it will. But I have to live with my mistakes. Can you?"

Harper studied her for a long moment. "You talk about consequences, Morgan, but have you ever stopped to wonder why you feel so guilty? Why you're consumed by this? You weren't the one who orchestrated the destruction. You weren't the one who manipulated people for your own gain."

Morgan clenched her fists. "I would have tried to stop it had I known."

"I'm sure," Harper said, her eyes flashing with something dark, something too old to be anger. "Although I've monitored you Morgan we didn't really know each other. But now you are complicit, whether you want to admit it or not. You were gonna bury the truth for money. Right? And now you're trying to make yourself the martyr, the 'good guy,' standing in my shadow with your new book."

"You think I wanted any of this?" Morgan's voice cracked, emotion bubbling beneath the surface. "You think I wanted to be a part of what you did? I wanted out as soon as I realized what you had done. I wanted out so badly, but I couldn't leave. You… you made me feel like I had no choice. All I wanted was to write the life story of someone I admired and looked up to. Little did I know how crazy you are!"

Harper's expression softened, but it was a cruel softness, a kind of recognition that stung worse than any mockery. "I did make you feel like that, didn't I? I made you feel like you were nothing without me. That the only thing worth living for was power, control and money. Truth? It is!"

Morgan said, "I don't want any of that anymore," the words tasting bitter. "I never really did. I just wanted out, but you—"

"I was your escape, Morgan," Harper interrupted, her voice sharp and intense. "You were willing to sacrifice everything—your dignity, your integrity, your soul—just to feel like you were somebody. I was your way out, and you chose to follow me. Every step, every turn, every decision… it was your choice. And now, you're trying to rewrite the story, but the truth is: you were always a part of it."

Morgan recoiled slightly, as if struck by a physical blow. The words stung, but it wasn't the cruelty in Harper's voice that hurt. It was the truth of them. She had been part of it. She had let Harper's darkness seep into her own life, and now, even after everything—after exposing Harper , after breaking free—Morgan couldn't outrun the stain. It was there, buried within her, a big sign of how far she'd fallen.

"You're right," Morgan whispered, tears welling up in her eyes. "I let you drag me down. I let you control me and I wanted the money. Now I don't know how to move on and leave this behind when every part of me feels like I've destroyed you."

"You have!" Harper looked at her, her face unreadable for a long moment. When she spoke again, her voice was quiet—almost too quiet. "It's hard, isn't it? To walk away from the wreckage when you're still covered in the ashes. We live with the scars, Morgan. The choices we make, the things we've done… they don't go away. We can't outrun them. No matter how far we run, they'll always be there, lingering in the dark."

"I don't know if I can live with it," Morgan said, the weight of the admission heavy in her chest. "I don't know if I can forgive you. I have nightmares now"

"You're not the first," Harper said, her voice hollow. "The world isn't kind to people like us. We destroy what we touches much as we create consumed by our own ambition for fame and fortune. But here's the thing about that—it never satisfies, not really. At some point, it has to give way to reality. The question is whether you'll be able to stand in it."

Her reflection in a darkened window caught her eye, and she saw for the first time the woman who had been standing in Harper's shadow for too long. She was not that woman anymore. She was different—

149

broken, yes, but still alive, still breathing. "I don't know if I can," Morgan whispered. "But I'll try."

Harper's lips curled, the hint of a smile that wasn't quite mocking, but something more complex. "Try, then. But remember this: good and evil... it's not as clear-cut as you think. We all have a little bit of both inside us. The only thing that matters is which side you choose when the moment comes."

Morgan didn't answer, only stared at the woman who had murdered for so long. In that silence, Morgan realized something profound: Harper wasn't the only one who had made choices. And it was Morgan, not Harper, who would decide what came next. The room fell into silence, the weight of their conversation hanging heavy in the air. It was Morgan's turn to speak, and this time, she knew exactly what to say. "You're not walkin!" Harper did not respond and after 5 minutes of silence Morgan got up and, without saying another word, left.

# CHAPTER 14

## The Unspoken Truth

Two weeks passed and she got another call from jail asking her to meet with Harper again. She did not know why but she agreed. The room was stiflingly quiet, the air thick with unspoken words. Morgan sat across from Harper her hands clenched tightly in her lap, heart pounding with an unsettling mix of anticipation and dread. It had been a few weeks since their last confrontation, weeks more since Harper had been arrested and the truth about her criminal empire had been exposed. Yet here they were, trapped together again in some new web of secrets.

Harper's face was unreadable, but her eyes—those eyes that Morgan had once trusted—now seemed distant, cold, and calculating. The space between them felt impossibly vast, filled with the ghosts of their shared past. Morgan could feel her own pulse echoing in her ears, the weight of Harper's stair was heavy, like a trap closing in around her.

Harper spoke first, her voice calm, almost conversational. "Do you ever wonder, Morgan, about the things we never talk about? The things we've buried so deep that even we can't remember them sometimes?"

Morgan shifted in her seat, her throat dry. She had no idea where this conversation was heading, but she knew it probably wouldn't be good. "What are you talking about?" she asked, her voice barely above a whisper.

Harper's lips curled slightly. "You've lived your whole life pretending that the past is just a series of mistakes—things you can correct, things you can fix. But some things can't be fixed, Morgan. Some things are just… done. Final."

Morgan narrowed her eyes, instinctively sensing that Harper was about to reveal something more consequential than anything she had shared before. "Don't fool around, What are you saying?"

Harper's eyes softened, almost in pity, as if Morgan were a child who simply didn't understand the weight of what was coming. "You remember that night, don't you? The one that changed everything for you. That night you killed someone?"

Morgan froze. The words hit her like a freight train, and for a moment, everything went black. Her mind raced, but she couldn't focus. The memories came flooding back, each one more fragmented and distorted than the last. She knew what Harper was now referring to. She had been at a party, a gathering with some friends—no, classmates. And she had fought. She had argued. But she hadn't—

"I didn't kill anyone," Morgan said, her voice sharp, but it trembled. "I didn't."

Harper's smile was cold, calculated. "You don't remember it, do you? You don't want to remember what happened that night."

The room seemed to close in around Morgan. She could feel her breath coming faster now, panic rising in her. "You're lying!"

"I'm not lying, Morgan and deep in your heart you know it," Harper said softly, her voice laced with something darker. "I was there. I saw it all. And I watched you do it."

Morgan's vision blurred for a moment as her mind tried to catch up with the implications of Harper's words. Her throat tightened. "What do you mean? I —I don't remember anything like that."

Harper leaned forward, her eyes never leaving Morgan's. "That's the thing, isn't it? Like we talked about before, memory can be a funny thing. It can protect you from the truth until you're ready to face it. But I was there. And I saw eeeeeeverything."

A shudder ran down Morgan's spine, her skin prickling with a cold sweat. She struggled to keep herself together, but the tension in the room made it impossible to think straight.

"What are you talking about?" Morgan demanded, her voice shaking now.

Harper didn't answer immediately. Instead, she stared at Morgan for a long, uncomfortable moment, as though she were savoring the discomfort she was causing. Then she spoke, her voice was low and almost nostalgic.

"It was a Thursday night, I remember. You were in your junior year at U of M, I had come to speak at the annual writer's symposium and later that night you were at a party with Brian— remember him? He was the one who always laughed too loud, tried to impress everyone with his stories. And you were fighting with his old girlfriend. You and Jessica. She was always the one who got under your skin, wasn't she? But you couldn't stop it that night. You were sooooo angry and you wanted to get even with her."

Morgan's heart skipped a beat. Brian. Jessica. Yes she knew those names, but the memories they belonged to were hazy, out of focus, like a dream she couldn't quite wake from. "I don't really

154

remember it was so long ago—what happened?"

There was a long pause. "You pushed her, Morgan. Right out the goddamn window," Harper said calmly. "Maybe you didn't mean to, but you did. You were fighting, she was sitting on the ledge and she fell three stories just like that. One second she was there, the next she was gone. You didn't even look down, did you? You just turned and walked away, like it was nothing. Honey you are the real killer not me!"

"No," Morgan gasped, her hands trembling now. She was shaking all over. This couldn't be true. It couldn't. She had never hurt anyone like that. She couldn't have, she thought to herself.

"You blotted it out and didn't remember it the next day either," Harper continued, her voice becoming more insistent, as though trying to force the memory back into Morgan's mind. "You didn't even realize she was gone until the police arrived, but I remember. I was right there that night. I saw everything. And afterward you couldn't remember a thing. I thought for sure you'd crack, but you didn't. With her death ruled a suicide you went with life like nothing happened. It was amazing."

Morgan's breathing grew erratic. Her chest was tight, her hands clammy. She wanted to scream, to tell Harper she was lying, that it was all some twisted joke—but deep down, a part of her knew that Harper wasn't lying. She could feel it in her bones, this gnawing sense of truth, the quiet realization that she had done something terrible back then, something irreversible.

"No," Morgan whispered, shaking her head violently. "I don't remember. I don't remember anything like that."

"That's the way it works, Morgan," Harper said softly, her tone almost tender now. "Memory is a shield. When the things you've done are too much to bear, your mind locks them away. But I was there. I remember. I never forgot."

Morgan's mind raced, her thoughts spinning in a blur of confusion. "But why didn't you say something? Why didn't you tell anyone?"

Harper tilted her head slightly, almost as if considering the question. "Why? Because you needed to live with it, Morgan. You needed to face the fact that you weren't the innocent victim you pretended to be. I knew it would come out eventually. I always knew. And you would have to live with it. Just like I have to and have had to for all these years."

"Just like you did?" Morgan echoed, her voice breaking. "What do you mean? What are you talking about?"

Harper sighed, sitting back in her chair. Her eyes grew distant, as if she were looking far beyond the walls of the room. "I've killed people, Morgan. More than you know. More than I care to count. And not just the ones with the Doctor. But you—you were the one who was special. You were the one who could understand. You didn't mean to do it, but you did. And I knew that you, of all people, would understand what it was like to carry that kind of guilt. I thought that you of all people would understand my guilt and what I did."

Morgan's was incensed. "You're sick," she spat, her voice trembling with anger and fear. "You're a damn monster!"

Harper's lips curved into a thin smile. "Maybe. Maybe I am. But I've lived with this darkness my entire life, Morgan. And now, I'm trying to give you a chance to understand. To see that we're not so different after all. I know you didn't want to hurt anyone, just like me. But sometimes, Morgan, things happen. People die. And all you can do is carry it, live with it, and keep on going."

Morgan's mind was reeling. She couldn't process what Harper was saying. It was too much. Her world felt like it was spinning, shifting, breaking apart. "You think I'd just forgive you for what you've done and the lives you've taken?"

"No more than Jessica's parents should forgive you. And besides I don't want your forgiveness," Harper said, her voice soft, almost regretful. "I want you to understand. I want you to see that I didn't choose this. It was thrust upon me, just like it was thrust upon you."

Morgan's heart was pounding, her hands shaking uncontrollably. "I didn't kill anyone. I didn't—"

"But you did," Harper interrupted, her voice sharp now, a dangerous edge creeping into her words. "Don't you get it? You definitely did and if you search your mind and heart, you will know it's true." Morgan's vision blurred as she felt the truth of Harper's words settle into her bones, like a poison slowly working its way through her system. She had never wanted this. She had never wanted to hurt anyone. All she wanted to do was write. And yet, the truth was undeniable. She had been complicit in something terrible, something monstrous. And Harper was right: she couldn't escape it. No matter how far she ran, the guilt would follow.

"I'm not like you," Morgan whispered, the words trembling in her throat.

Harper's eyes narrowed, almost pitying. "Maybe not. But we're both running from the same thing, Morgan. Our past. The same darkness. You can't outrun it. No one can."

The room fell into a heavy silence, the weight of their shared guilt hanging between them like a cloud. Morgan's mind was spinning, the words echoing in her ears, drowning out everything else. She wanted to scream, to run, to escape. But she couldn't. Not anymore.

Harper was right. They were both prisoners of their past. And now that the truth was at the forefront, there was no way out.

# CHAPTER 15

## A Dark Choice

The silence between them was deafening. Morgan sat across from Harper, her hands trembling slightly despite her best efforts to keep composed. The room seemed to shrink, the walls pressing in, as if the very air was heavy with the weight of the truth that was about to be revealed. Harper's eyes were cold and knowing, locked onto Morgan with a piercing intensity that made her skin crawl. Harper was now in the 6th week of her trail with closing arguments scheduled for the following week.

Morgan felt a deep unease settle in her stomach, an instinct telling her that whatever Harper was about to say would shatter everything she thought she knew about the woman sitting before her.

Harper tilted her head, her lips curling into a small, almost amused smile. "You're still trying to figure me out, aren't you? Still trying to understand what makes me tick."

"I don't care to understand you, I'll save that for the Doctor's," Morgan retorted, her voice shaky but defiant. "I don't care what kind of monster you are. I just want to know why. Why did you do all of this? Why couldn't you let the past lay and live me alone? Why didn't you just stop?"

Harper leaned back in her chair, crossing her arms in a gesture of comfort, as if she had prepared for this moment. She didn't seem fazed by Morgan's anger, as if she had expected it. Her gaze softened, but there was no warmth in her eyes. Only something cold, something unyielding.

"Stop?" Harper repeated, her voice carrying a dark amusement. "You still don't get it, do you? I can't stop. Because, Morgan, I don't want to stop. I like it!"

Morgan felt a cold shiver running through her. "What are you talking about? You're sick. You've been manipulating everyone around you, killing people... for what? What could possibly make you do something like that?"

Harper's eyes darkened, a glint of something dangerous flashing behind them. She leaned forward slowly, her voice dropping to a low, chilling whisper. "Enjoyment! You think I'm sick? You think I'm some twisted monster who kills for no reason?" She paused, as if savoring the moment. "No, Morgan. I kill because I love it."

Morgan's heart stopped. The words seemed to hang in the air, heavy and suffocating, and her mind struggled to comprehend the enormity of what Harper had just said. "What do you mean, you love it?"

Harper smiled, her eyes glimmering with an almost unsettling sense of satisfaction. "You don't understand yet, do you? You never did. You always thought that you were the good one, the one who could stay pure. But you're wrong. Everyone has a breaking point, Morgan. Everyone has a line they can't cross. I've crossed it, and now I live in it. I revel in it. Since that night I watched you from afar all these years and I knew that someday this day would come."

Morgan's voice faltered as she tried to process the words. "You're a monster."

CRIME SCENE DO NOT CROSS

Harper's smile didn't fade. "Maybe. Or maybe I'm just someone who understands something about the mind that you never will." Her voice took on a more reflective tone. "Do you know what it feels like, Morgan? To have all the power in the world, to control everything, to take someone's life and feel nothing but exhilaration?"

Morgan recoiled, her stomach turning. "No. I don't."

Harper's eyes narrowed, locking onto her with an intensity that sent a jolt of fear through Morgan. "You should. You should understand it. You're not so different from me. You've always wanted control, haven't you? You've always wanted to feel like you were in charge of your own fate. But you can't. Not really. Not unless you're willing to take it, to make it yours."

Morgan shook her head, her chest tightening with a mix of revulsion and confusion. "I would never... I would never hurt someone. I'm not like you."

Harper let out a soft laugh, almost pitying, as if she were humoring a child. "You think I'm so different from you? You think you could never become like me? You think I just woke up one day and decided to start killing?" She leaned in closer, her voice dropping to a deadly whisper. "No, Morgan. It was the power that drew me in. The power of life and death. The power of making someone disappear with a single decision, a single moment. Do you know what that feels like? To control someone's destiny with just the snap of your fingers?"

Morgan's mouth went dry. She couldn't speak. She didn't want to hear any more. But Harper wasn't finished.

"It's intoxicating, Morgan, it's an addiction," Harper continued, her voice almost reverent now, her eyes distant as though she were reliving the very act. "You start to crave it. The control, the rush. Every time you take another life, it's like a drug, a high you can't ever get enough of. It doesn't matter who they are, what they've done. All that matters is that you have the power. And when you realize that— when you understand it and come to appreciate it— you will never go back."

Morgan's heart pounded in her chest, her hands clammy as she fought to hold onto her sense of reality. "I'm not like you. I'll never be like you," she whispered, more to herself than to Harper.

The veteran author and soon to be convicted felon's expression softened slightly, but it was far from sympathetic. "You say that now. But you don't understand what it's like to live with that kind of power. When you're in control, when you can make someone's life unravel with the snap of your fingers, there's no going back. You're addicted. We're both trapped in this web of our own making. But you... you of all people should understand. You've always been so close to crossing that line. You just haven't realized it yet."

Morgan shook her head, fighting the overwhelming sense of dread crawling under her skin. "I don't want that power. I don't want to become like you."

Harper's smile was small but undeniably satisfied. "That's where you're wrong. You already are. The difference between us is that I've embraced it. I've taken it and made it mine. And you're still pretending it's not there. But deep down, Morgan, you know it is. You know that if you had the chance, you would have done the same thing I did. Maybe not yet, maybe not in the same way. But given the right circumstances... You could and would have."

The words hit Morgan like a prizefighter. She wanted to deny it. She wanted to scream, to run or to fight back against the accusation. But deep down, a small, uncomfortable voice whispered that Harper might be right. She had always felt a hunger for control, for power. But she had never acted on it.

Yet, the thought lingered, like a seed being planted deep in her mind, rooting itself in the dark corners of her thoughts. The feeling of absolute control... Was it possible? Was Harper right?

"Why are you telling me all of this?" Morgan finally asked, her voice barely audible. Her heart raced, and the world around her seemed to blur. "Why now?"

Harper's eyes softened, and for the briefest moment, Morgan saw something vulnerable, something almost human behind the cold, calculating exterior. "Because, Morgan, you need to understand that power isn't something you can walk away from. It's something you have to own. And you're the only person who can understand that, because you're the only person I've ever known who has it in them to do what I did."

Morgan looked at Harper, her mind reeling, her emotions torn between disgust and a strange, twisted curiosity. She wanted to hate her, to believe that she was entirely different from this woman. But a part of her couldn't shake the fear that perhaps, deep down, Harper was right. And that was the scariest thought of all.

"Maybe I'll never be like you," Morgan whispered, her voice barely audible. "But I'll never forget what you've done. What you've made me question."
Harper's sight never left her, her smile growing wider, almost triumphant. "You don't need to be like me, Morgan. Not yet. But the truth is, you'll never be able to forget. And that, in itself, is the power I've now given you."

The room was heavy with silence as Morgan absorbed Harper's words, the weight of them sinking deep into her soul. She didn't know what to think, didn't know what to believe. But she knew one thing for certain and that was that Harper had opened a door that Morgan could never fully close again.

Harper's manipulative and twisted psyche, revealed how she uses power and control to ensnare people feeding their doubts and fears. Morgan was struggling to reconcile her own beliefs with the darkness that Harper embodied.

The rain beat against the windows like a thousand tiny drums, a rhythmic, steady percussion that matched the pace of Morgan's thoughts. Inside the

room, the air was thick with tension, an almost tangible force that made every breath feel heavy, every movement deliberate. Harper sat across from her, as calm and poised as ever, her eyes glinting with an unreadable expression, as if she were waiting for Morgan to make a move.

Morgan could feel the weight of the decision pressing on her chest, each second ticking by with the promise of something irreversible. She had been pacing the room, her mind a whirlwind of conflicting thoughts, but one truth had remained constant throughout. Harper was too dangerous and Morgan knew it. She knew it deep down in the pit of her stomach.

Harper's smile was small but knowing, as if she had somehow anticipated this moment. Her gaze never left Morgan, studying her with an unsettling intensity that made Morgan's skin crawl.

"You're thinking about it," Harper said, her voice soft but carrying an edge of amusement. "You're wondering whether you could do it, aren't you?"

Morgan stopped pacing and turned to face her, her heart pounding in her chest. She couldn't look away from Harper's piercing gaze, the cold, calculating eyes that had seen through her from the moment they'd met. Harper had always known more than Morgan was willing to admit, always read her better than anyone else ever could.

"No," Morgan said, her voice barely a whisper. "I'm not thinking about it."

Harper's smile widened, but it wasn't kind. It wasn't a smile of understanding, but a smile of recognition. She knew. She knew exactly what Morgan was struggling with, and she knew that Morgan was just a few moments away from making a choice that would haunt her forever.

"You don't have to lie to me, Morgan," Harper said, her voice low and almost tender. "You've been thinking about it for months. You've been wondering how to stop me. How to end this. How to keep your own secret safe."

Morgan felt a chill run down her spine. The words struck too close to home, and for a moment, she couldn't breathe. Harper was right. She had been thinking about it—thinking about how to stop the one person who was a bonded killer and knew her darkest secrets. She wanted to know how to stop the one person who would never hesitate to kill again, to hurt again, to use the power of manipulation to destroy everyone and anyone in her path.

And Morgan knew, deep in her gut, that Harper would never stop. If she was convicted and she ever got out she would kill again for sure. She could always find someone to exploit, someone to control, someone to use as a pawn in her sick, need to fulfill her murderous cravings. The thought made Morgan's blood run cold. But there was something else, too. Something darker.

What if Harper wasn't wrong? What if Morgan did need to do this? What if there was no other way out? If Harper lived, she would continue to manipulate, to kill, to play her games—and Morgan's life would never be the same. The guilt, the fear of being found out, would eat away at her every day, every hour, every minute.

She had already crossed a line when she had kept Harper's secret. The whispers in her head grew louder, telling her that the only way to keep herself safe, to keep her secret safe, was to end this before it spiraled out of control even further. Before Harper could destroy everything Morgan had worked so hard to build.

"You don't have to do this," Harper said softly, almost coaxingly. "You don't have to be like me."

Morgan's hands trembled slightly, her mind a war zone of conflicting emotions. She had spent so long running from the truth, hiding from it, trying to pretend that she wasn't capable of something like this. But Harper was right: she had always been close. She had always wanted control, wanted power, wanted to be the one in charge. What had stopped her before was fear. But now... now she wasn't sure if it was fear anymore.

"No, Ms. Harper," Morgan said, her voice steady, but the words felt foreign on her tongue. "I don't have to be like you. But I do have to stop you."

Harper's eyes narrowed slightly, a flicker of something almost like disappointment flashing across her face. "I see. So this is how it ends then. You're going to try and kill me?"

Morgan didn't answer at first. She couldn't. She was still grappling with the weight of the decision, still trying to push away the rising tide of nausea that threatened to overwhelm her. She wasn't a killer. She never had been. She had lived a life built on carefully controlled choices and calculated risks. She had buried the events of that fateful night and she prided herself on keeping the darkness at bay.

But Harper had pushed her to this point, had forced her to make a choice between survival and complicity. Morgan felt cornered into making a choice to preserve her own safety and ensure Harper could no longer harm anyone else.

"You think it's easy?" Morgan said, the words slipping out before she could stop them. "You think this is some kind of game? That I want to kill you?" She shook her head. "No, Harper . I'm doing this because I have no choice. Because you won't stop."

Harper studied her for a long moment, her expression unreadable. Then, to Morgan's surprise, she laughed—a soft, almost amused sound that only made Morgan's stomach twist more with discomfort.

"You really believe that?" Harper asked, her voice almost too calm. "You think you have no choice? That you're doing this for some higher reason? You're just like me, Morgan. You're doing this because you want control. Because you need to."

"No," Morgan said, her voice low and steady. "I'm doing this because it's the only way to protect myself. To protect everyone else you could destroy. I can't let you keep doing this."

Harper's smile faded, but the look in her eyes grew darker, sharper. "You really think you'll get away with it? You really think you'll walk away from this without it changing you? Without it leaving a mark on your soul?"

"I'm not walking away from anything," Morgan replied, her voice unwavering. "This is the end. For both of us."

There was a pause, an exhale of breath as the two women faced each other in the stillness of the visiting room. Time seemed to slow, each second stretching into eternity as Morgan's heart beat loudly in her chest, each thud a reminder of the irreversible choice she was about to make.

Harper leaned back in her chair, her eyes never leaving Morgan's. "You're a fool if you think you can just move on after this. You're a fool if you think this will make you any different from me."

Morgan swallowed, the weight of the decision pressing on her chest like a thousand pounds. But she had made up her mind. Harper had left her no choice. There was no other way. She would stop Harper, no matter what it took. And she would do it now.

"So how do you aim to kill me?" Harper asked.

"I already have!" responded Morgan with a smile.

"How so?" inquired Harper.

"You know that coffee you drank about 45 minutes ago? I put a rare and undetectable poison in it and in another hour or so you will become paralyzed and by tonight? You'll be dead!" she explained. Morgan had gotten the poison from her fellow author Ethan Cole an expert at killing with substances. Morgan's eyes locked onto Harper's, as if she were watching a final act unfold. Her eyes widened, but Harper didn't scream.

Harper tried to talk but the poison had robbed her of her speech earlier than expected. She didn't fight back. She simply looked at Morgan with a mixture of fear and disbelief, as if she couldn't quite comprehend the full meaning of what was happening to her. Just then the second effects of the poison hit Harper's body and she collapsed on the floor and began to convulse with white foam forming at the edge of her mouth. It was not a glamour look for someone who had tried to look good her whole life. Morgan thought to herself that she was really looking forward to the funeral and making sure Harper could never kill again.

She thought about calling the guards but then thought better of it. She wasn't proud of it but found that she was enjoying watching her die.

"Goodbye Vivian," Morgan whispered to her, the words had a satisfying feel to them.

And as Harper lay on the floor and her life began slipping away in earnest, so too did the last remnants of Morgan's imagined innocence. She was a full blown killer now.

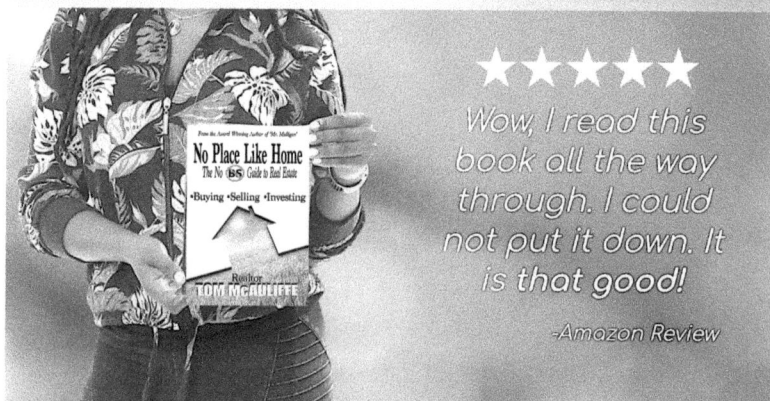

# ACKNOWLEDGEMENTS

The Harvill Foundation

Professor Dale L Roberts

The Team at Draft 2 Digital

Danielle Dyball, Editorial Services

Some Images from DepositPhotos.com

# <u>Please Leave a Review!</u>

## *A Small Ask...*

*Now that you've finished reading this book, what do you think of what you read? Are there any tips or information you found insightful? What do you think is missing from this book? While you're thinking back on what you read, it'd mean the world to me if you left an honest review online or send us an email.*

*As you probably know, reviews play a part in building relevancy for all products online. Whether you found the information enjoyable or worthless, your candid review helps others make an informed purchase.*
*Also, based on your review, I'll adjust this publication and future editions.*

*I appreciate your support!*

*Tom*

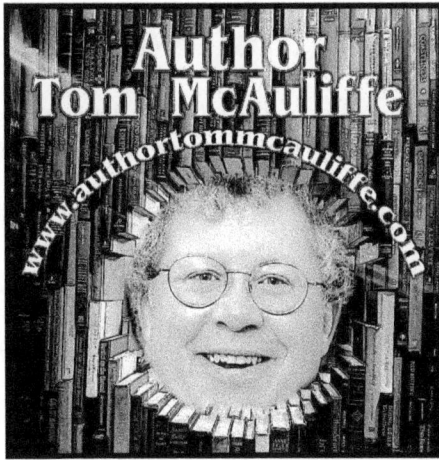

## Please send questions to:

*Bookinfo@nextstopparadise.com*

## *Member:*

Alliance of Independent Authors

Emerald Coast Writers

Military Photojournalists Association

Florida Writers Association

Alliance of Independent Authors

# Books By Author Tom McAuliffe

- Mr. Mulligan - *The Life of Champion Armless Golfer Tommy McAuliffe*

- Nuts! - *The Life & Times of Gen. Tony McAuliffe*

- Throttle Up - *Astronaut Teacher Christa McAuliffe*

- Mad Dog! - *Detroit Tiger Dick McAuliffe*

- Charmed - *From Motown to Combat & Back*

- Almost - *The Road to the Grande*

- Thunder Road - *Goodyear, God & Gatorade*

- Buddy, Brian and Me - *A Spooky Rock Story*

- Frozen - *A WWII and Mind over Matter Tale*

- Soft Shell - *Teddy the Talking Turtle*

- Max and Me - *Paws Across The Water*

- Off the Rock - *Escaping Alcatraz*

- Deepwater Oil - *Drillin on the Moon*

- Who Won? - *The 2024 Presidential Election*

- No Place Like Home - *The No BS RE Guide*

- The Lake - *Divided Waters*

- Death on the Page - *Revenge on the Reviewer*

- Oracle - *The Algorithmic Age*

- Murder in the Margins - *Blood on the Page*

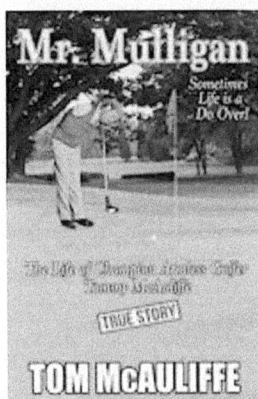

- **Books**

- **eBooks**

- **Audiobooks**

*Available at most online outlets
and your favorite bookstore!*

*Also Available at:*

# WWW.AUTHORTOMMCAULIFFE.COM

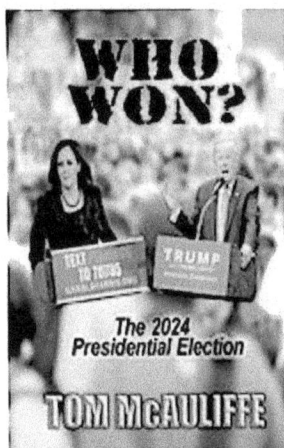

WHO WON?
The 2024 Presidential Election
TOM McAULIFFE

TOM McAULIFFE
DEEP WATER OIL
DRILLIN' ON THE MOON

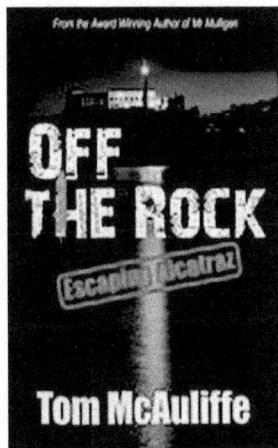

From the Award Winning Author of Mr Mulligan
OFF THE ROCK
Escaping Alcatraz
Tom McAuliffe

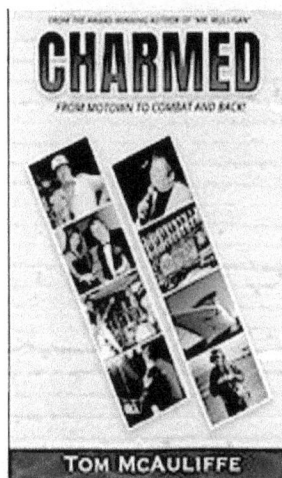

CHARMED
FROM MOTOWN TO COMBAT AND BACK!
TOM McAULIFFE

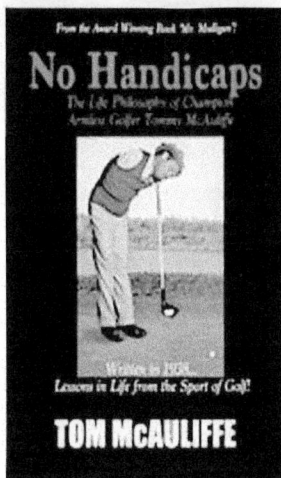

From the Award Winning Book 'Mr. Mulligan?'
No Handicaps
The Life Philosophy of Champion
Amateur Golfer Tommy McAuliffe
Written in 1958.
Lessons in Life from the Sport of Golf!
TOM McAULIFFE

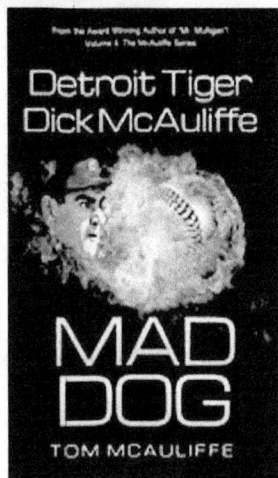

From the Award Winning Author of 'Mr. Mulligan'
Volume 6 The McAuliffe Series
Detroit Tiger
Dick McAuliffe
MAD DOG
TOM McAULIFFE

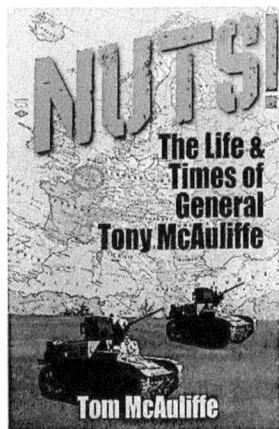

NUTS!
The Life & Times of General Tony McAuliffe
Tom McAuliffe

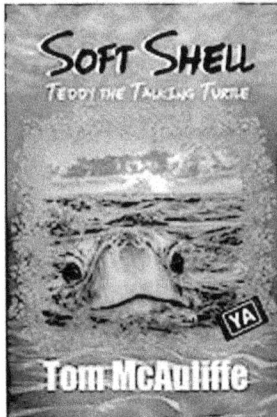

SOFT SHELL
TEDDY THE TALKING TURTLE
YA
Tom McAuliffe

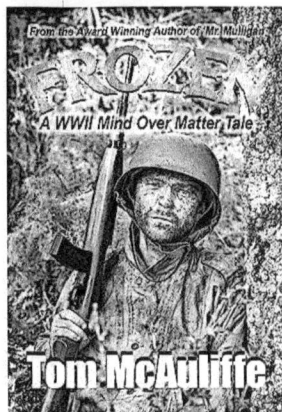

From the Award Winning Author of 'Mr. Mulligan'
FROZEN
A WWII Mind Over Matter Tale
Tom McAuliffe

A NEW PSYCHOLOGICAL THRILLER
FOR 2025!

written by humans
not by AI

www.ingramcontent.com/pod-product-compliance
Ingram Content Group UK Ltd.
Pitfield, Milton Keynes, MK11 3LW, UK
UKHW021021100125
453365UK00012B/607

9 798230 356936